D1331107

A NIGHT IN
HALLOWEEN HOUSE

Elyse Willems

CHAPTER 1

Baseball

"That was a strike and you know it!"

Billy threw down his baseball mitt and kicked at the graveled ground, wishing he was standing on an actual pitcher's mound instead of a patch of overgrown weeds. Most talents came naturally to him, pitching included, but this afternoon he was hurling duster after duster.

Some twenty feet away at bat stood Jeremy, commonly known to all but his parents and teachers as "Germ." Not a bad kid, but prone to mischief when left to his own devices. Small in size, what Germ lacked in height he made up for in snark, attitude, and biting quips.

"A *strike*?! Are you blind? That was a ball. Back me up, Chuck!" Germ gave an amused snort. "Ha! 'Up-Chuck!' Get it?"

Chuck, the unattentive catcher, was preoccupied with a colony of ants digging a tunnel beneath the makeshift home plate. "Looked good to me," he replied, absentmindedly. Using one stubby, grubby finger, Chuck pushed his thick glasses up his nose, and restored his attention to the ants. A gentle soul, what Chuck lacked in athletic prowess he made up for in always having the best snacks in his book bag, and an eagerness to share.

"Geez, can we get on with it already?" A voice called from the outfield. "Dad said if I'm home by seven I can watch *MacGuyer*." The voice belonged to Phil, and Phil was lying. It was his mother, the time was eight, and the show was *Weekly Science Hour*. As the resident geek of the group, Phil's tastes in TV and bookish interests were no secret. Even so, his friends could get on his case from time-to-time. Not to mention he was the only kid on the block who wore a button-up shirt and pocket protector to the baseball diamond.

It was a warmer than average fall afternoon and what would ultimately be the last pick-up game of the season. And what a season it had been! Attendance was exemplary, save for the week when Phil went to science camp, and Germ's mother only forced him to bring his younger visiting cousin Margot, twice ("she can play 'left-out'").

The four boys had been friends for years. Billy and Chuck met in elementary school, Phil and Billy were next door neighbors, and none could recall life before Germ. Regardless, this summer had solidified the crew's friendship. That, and some pretty fierce trash-talk.

"Get ready for the heat!" Billy stood pin straight, solemnly eyeing imaginary runners on first and third. Matching his intensity, Germ planted his feet and tightened his grip on the rusted bat. Phil kneaded his fist into his glove, and good ol' Chuck kept one eye on the action and the other on the ants.

Inhaling deeply, Billy wound up. Giving it his all, he flung the baseball toward home plate. What resulted was a perfect pitch;

Germ was instantly taken aback by the speed of the ball, not to mention how it sliced directly down the center of the field. Teeth gritted, he closed his eyes and swung as hard as he could. Bat met ball and a loud, reverberating CRACK sounded. Upon opening his eyes, Germ was surprised to see the ball sailing overhead. Instead of running to first base, he hung back, watching his handiwork with pure self-admiration. Billy, mouth agape, observed with shocked dismay and let his mitt fall limply off his hand. The hit was so impressive that even Chuck took a brief moment to look up from the ants and marvel at this exceptional display of athleticism.

Late afternoon sun bore directly into Phil's eyes as he struggled to get under the ball and make the catch. It didn't matter that he was the tallest of the crew, or how far he extended his glove overhead; the ball moved further out of reach, soaring higher and higher. So high, that it left the safety of the field, breaching the top of the worn wooden fence. Passing over shrubs and a thicket of brambles, bouncing and rolling until coming to its final resting place. Deep in the yard beyond the fence.

The yard of Bryerwood House.

CHAPTER 2

Don't Look Back

"**N**ot it!" Germ shouted, abandoning the game and making a move toward the collective pile of knapsacks and bikes.

Billy ran over and threw himself in front of Germ, blocking his friend's path. Size was no contest here, as Billy towered over Germ. Nevertheless, the two had fought before and Germ was surprisingly cagey.

"Don't you dare, Germ! You know the rules. You hit the ball out, YOU go get it."

"Phil's the one who didn't catch it," Germ protested, his jaw clenched.

Phil's eyes bugged out of his head. "And how by Newton's Law did you expect me to catch that? With a ladder?"

"It was a pretty great hit, wasn't it?" Germ smirked.

"Pretty great... if it wasn't our last ball," said Phil, shaking his head.

Chuck peered out from under his oversized cap and pushed up his glasses. "If you think about it, 'makes most sense for Germ and

Bill to go together!" he proclaimed.

Billy and Germ spun and glared at Chuck.

"You can't be bothered to pay attention to the game, but now you've a sudden interest?" barked Germ. Poor Chuck shrugged, apologetic.

"He's not wrong," said Phil. "Looking at this logically, we can identify and directly correlate who's responsible." Phil approached every situation as if it were a puzzle waiting to be solved. "Billy threw the ball, and Germ, you hit it. Chuck and I were basically bystanders. And, it goes without saying, but I *told* you we shouldn't play near Bryerwood House."

"Keep your voice down!" hissed Germ, half-whispering. "And way to rub it in, Phil. You know we couldn't play at the park... Chuck's brother and his cronies would've given us atomic wedgies so bad we'd have gone nuclear."

Chuck stared at his shoes, his plump cheeks reddening. It was bad enough that his older brother Nick terrorized him on a daily basis, but things were much worse when "Noogie Nick" and his friends got a hold of the boys. A few years older and several streaks meaner, Nick and his goons didn't care that Chuck was a blood relative, often making him a primary torture target.

Billy took notice of Chuck's downtrodden expression and felt a pang of guilt. It wasn't Chuck's fault that his brother was a raging bully and total sociopath.

"The park sucks anyway," said Billy. "The Bryerwood lot is much closer to the arcade."

Chuck shot him a timid, appreciative smile. Billy smiled back, then clapped his hands together. "Alright, c'mon Germ. Let's go. You and me. We're getting that ball back."

Germ rolled his eyes. "Fine. I'll go. Getting murdered in that house will give me an excuse for failing math." He turned to the other boys. "Phil, you and Chuck stand and keep watch. And if anything happens-"

"- Run screaming and don't look back. Got it," Phil nodded.

CHAPTER 3

The Bryerwood House

The Bryerwood House was the scariest place in town.

Located on a quaint cul-de-sac, it towered over the other picturesque family homes. Flanked on either side by a thick growth of trees and bramble, Bryerwood stood out like a sore thumb, a dark, solitary fortress, gothically defiant in the face of pastel cookie-cutter suburbia. Decades had passed since anyone was last seen going into or leaving the property. In fact, it had been so long that no one could even remember who the last owners were. The locals made up stories about unwitting prospective buyers who - after only minutes inside - fled the place screaming; families looking to settle down in an otherwise tight-knit community, or investors hoping to flip and turn a quick buck. Always a horrific or tragic tale, and ranging from ghost story to creature feature to demonic possession.

It was commonly accepted among the neighborhood kids that you didn't go past Bryerwood House at night, since strange stuff was reported to happen there. Some of the littler kids wouldn't even ride their bikes past it during the day. And everyone knew, no matter how tempting it looked, not to play in the vacant lot near the fence.

Despite this, Billy and his friends had ignored all warnings and abandoned common sense. Now they stood shoulder-to-shoulder at the foot of the driveway, staring up at the looming monolith before them. Germ gave it a hard look, then crossed his arms and shook his head.

"I don't see why we have to go in through the front yard. Lemme climb the fence, I'll have it in no time."

"You can climb the fence, sure, but you'll get caught in the vines," Phil said, matter-of-factly.

Billy tightened his grip on the rusty baseball bat. If he was going in, he was going in armed. "At least it's a straight shot if we go through the front."

Phil pointed to the west side of the house. "By my estimate, the ball should be somewhere within that area."

"But what if someone sees you?" asked Chuck, biting his lip.

"I'll tell 'em to take a picture, it'll last longer," Germ spat.

"There's no one in there. Hasn't been for years." Billy said the words confidently, though he didn't necessarily believe them. He gave Germ a nudge and gestured toward the house. "Let's go."

Taking a deep breath, Billy willed himself forward, crossing the threshold between the curb and the Bryerwood property. Slowly, he entered the yard, Germ following behind, his eyes scanning wildly. Chuck and Phil looked on, helpless, like puppies who watch their owners leave for work, unconvinced that they'll ever return.

A tall and tarnished wrought iron fence surrounded the property. With trepidation, Billy gave the gate a push. Slowly it lurched back, groaning in anguish, the sound of years of neglect.

Billy exchanged an uneasy look with Germ, then stepped through the gate.

The yard was untamed, overgrown with weeds and covered in fallen tree branches and other debris. Dark and cloaked in shadow, it felt like a completely different world compared to the sunny suburban yards that surrounded it. Even the dense forest of plants and trees that lined the walk resembled a foreign species, the exotic and dangerous flora you'd find in the recesses of the Amazon. Billy took notice of one distinctively mean looking shrub that looked like it would fight back if provoked. His mind wandered as he considered what wrestling a mean shrub might look like, though he didn't want to find out.

Germ trailed closely behind and Billy could hear his friend breathing rapidly. Due to his height, Germ was having a trickier time navigating some of the higher brush. Quick to tout himself as the tough one of the group, Germ wasn't above teasing Chuck for his insecurities. That being said, Billy could almost feel Germ shivering next to him, despite it being fairly warm out.

"Look, the path branches ahead here. If we hang left, it'll take us to the side the ball landed on," Germ whispered intensely.

Billy nodded. "Okay, but keep your voice down -- someone might hear you."

"Who? The Boogeyman?" Germ laughed, but Billy could tell from the sound of his voice his friend was on edge. Billy was too; jokes aside, the Boogeyman didn't seem so far fetched right now.

The boys took the path forking to the left. As they rounded the house, Billy noticed its crumbling facade. The siding was so dirty it was impossible to tell what the original paint job was. Not to mention the surrounding trees played tricks with the light.

The architecture was turn-of-the-century Victorian Gothic, and stuck out like a sore thumb in the sea of quaint bungalows. Large and imposing, with steep gables and pointed spires, not a sign of life could be seen from the outside, as the windows were either barricaded with wooden boards, covered in layers of dirt, or shrouded by dark curtains. Rotting stairs led to a wraparound porch, the centerpiece of which was a dark, dark foreboding door. A door that appeared as if it hadn't been opened in a long time, and, should you open it, you wouldn't like what you found on the other side. The rarest baseball card in the world couldn't convince Billy to open that door and go inside.

Treading softly on tiptoe, the boys reached the spot where Phil predicted the ball would be. They scanned the area, and Billy's heart fell in his chest when reality set in.

There was no ball.

CHAPTER 4

Ghosts

"W-where is it?" Germ stammered. "Phil SAID it would be here. And he's-

"-Never wrong, I know," Billy said, finishing Germ's sentence. He also couldn't believe his eyes. They'd seen the ball fall and it was very unlikely that it got stuck in a tree, or wedged elsewhere. Plus the grass wasn't too high here, mostly dirt.

Without disturbing the area, the boys searched. And searched. Five minutes felt like fifty. Until finally Germ threw in the towel.

"It's getting dark, Bill. The streetlamps are on. We've gotta go." Normally Germ was the one pushing the others to stay out just a little later and break curfew, so this was a first. "I might have an extra ball in my garage, trapped behind some old tires or something."

Billy nodded in agreement. "I hate to say it, but... you're right Germ. Let's go."

The boys turned to head back to the street, when they were startled by a loud *BANG* sound. Diving for cover, they hid behind the trunk of a wide oak tree.

"What was that?!" Germ reflexively grabbed at Billy's arm. "Where did it come from? Is someone else here?!"

Cautiously, Billy peered around the tree. He could see no one, however the sun was dipping lower and the house cast an expanding shadow over the yard.

"Phil? Chuck? Is that you?" He managed to say, his voice just above a croak.

Silence. No response. Billy turned to Germ and shrugged. Germ flapped his arms exasperated and shook his head. Billy made a motion to leave the security of the tree, and Germ begrudgingly followed, frowning.

They crept now, rounding the side of the house, heading back the direction they came. The surrounding brush was so thick that, coupled with the fading sunlight, the street was no longer visible.

As he and Germ rounded the porch, Billy couldn't help himself. Curiosity was eating away at him, and he had to see. Against every logical thought telling him not to, he glanced back at the dark foreboding door of Bryerwood House. What he saw shook him to his very core.

The door was now wide open.

Billy gasped. "Germ, s-someone else is... is *here*," he stammered.

Germ swiveled to see the open door. The last remaining color drained from his face and his mouth fell agape.

"You've got to be sh-"

Suddenly, like a shockwave hitting, an invisible force SLAMMED the door shut. And that was all it took.

Screaming at the top of their lungs, Billy and Germ took off through the yard, running for their young lives. Despite having placed third in this year's track and field meet, ths speed at which Billy ran would have put his winning score to shame. A few feet behind was Germ, dodging fallen tree trunks and prickly plants at a lightning pace, second only to the time he was late for curfew and his mother was threatening to confiscate his computer games.

They ran and ran, not even stopping once they hit the street. Phil and Chuck, albeit confused at first, quickly got the memo and followed.

None of them dared look back. And, because they didn't look back, they didn't see the solitary figure quietly watching from the window of Bryerwood.

CHAPTER 5

Bumps in the Night

That evening Billy was unusually subdued during supper, but his parents didn't seem to notice. He silently picked at his food, absent of any real appetite. It was customary for him and his dad to spend Sunday evenings working on model planes, but not tonight. Instead he joined his mother in the living room to watch TV, hoping it would take his mind off things. Billy sat glued to the couch, transfixed by an episode of The Twilight Zone called "The Shadow Man." It told the story of a boy who discovers a sinister man living under his bed, the titular "Shadow Man," who at first doesn't seem harmless. In typical Twilight Zone fashion, there's a dark twist and the Shadow Man's true nature is revealed..

Billy's mother rolled her eyes as they watched, denouncing this "new" episode. She claimed the classic series was better and this rebooted series was a lame ploy to exploit nostalgia. Meanwhile, Billy - frozen to the couch cushions with fear - couldn't help but wonder if a Shadow Man had followed him home from Bryerwood and was waiting beneath his bed, dark deeds in mind.

Sweaty and unnerved, Phil took a moment to compose himself before entering his house. Once inside he found his parents engaged in a high stakes match of the strategy game Go. His mother offered to put on the last few minutes of *Weekly Science Hour*, but Phil declined, heading straight for his room under the guise of having some last minute homework to finish. A quickly-crafted lie, since Phil's homework was always completed well in advance. Once in his room, Phil retrieved a spiral-bound notebook from his desk drawer and began to list in detail every piece of scientific evidence he could think of that debunked the existence of ghosts, monsters, and the paranormal.

The first thing Germ noticed when he got home was that his dad's car wasn't in the driveway. Back Friday from a business trip, his dad had promised he'd be in town through the following weekend. When Germ went inside he found his mom in the kitchen, her eyes red and puffy as if she'd been crying. Momentarily forgetting about Bryerwood House and his fears, Germ gave his mother a hug. As troublesome as Germ could be, the rest of the evening he was on his best behavior, helping with the remainder of dinner prep and clean-up, and acting the jester to make his mom laugh. He even kept the bickering with his sister to a minimum - not an easy feat.

Some ten blocks away, Chuck ran up his porch hyperventilating and flung open the screen door like a bat out of hell. The ruckus startled his grandmother who was mid-snooze in her easy chair. She awoke with a snort and clasped a hand over her mouth to avoid spitting out her dentures. Chuck proceeded to tell his grandmother about everything; the baseball, Bryerwood House, the narrow escape. She listened intently, as she always did. When he was done, she spoke in a grave voice, assuring Chuck that this was a terrifying ordeal. Disturbing, even for grandmothers. Why, just hearing him retell it shook her to her very core! Perhaps, she said, it wouldn't be out of the question for Chuck to get his sleeping bag and have a campout in her room that night? That way Chuck could protect *her* from any foul ghouls and fiends who might prey upon them?

Chuck was secretly elated as he was dreading the thought of going to sleep alone. So he very bravely accepted. There was nothing he wouldn't do for his Gram.

THOMP. While digging through his closet looking for a sleeping bag, Chuck was startled by the sound of steel-toed boots kicking open the screen door. Only one person around Chuck's house wore those; his brother, Noogie Nick.

Moving fast, he found the sleeping bag and made his way down the hall to his grandmother's suite, narrowly avoiding a confrontation with his bullying brother. And the bullet was dodged indeed. As Chuck turned the corner he could overhear staccato stomps nearing his bedroom door. Nick, likely in a bad mood and on the hunt for a human punching bag, paced, searching for his younger brother. With no sign of his target, Nick soon gave up. Chuck exhaled a sigh of relief.

That night Billy left the light on for the first time in years, though no amount of light could shield his imagination from the horrible things that lurked in the dark.

Sleep came eventually for the boys, but so did the nightmares. Visions of long, black, talon-like fingers wrapping, clutching, dragging them into the Bryerwood House. Ghosts and ghouls, monsters of all shapes and sizes swallowed them up, pulling them deeper into the shadowy recesses. A thousand sets of hands reached out smothering their muffled screams, clawing and thrashing. Eventually, the ominous dark door slammed shut once more. Only this time, it trapped the boys in the house for good.

CHAPTER 6

Replacement

Billy found it hard to focus in class the next morning. Distracted by the events of the day prior and still reeling from his dreams, he hadn't yet had a chance to sit down with his friends and talk through what happened. Usually Billy and Phil rode bikes to school together, but Phil was running late so Billy went on his own.

Now he sat in third period social studies watching the clock. The moment the bell sounded, Billy grabbed his bag and leapt from his seat in one swift motion, gunning it for the cafeteria.

Sure enough, the other boys had done the exact same thing. Taking their seats at the usual corner table, they eyed one another anxiously. Everyone looked tired and disturbed, coming off a sleepless night. After a few tense moments, Billy broke the silence.

"Trespassing was a bad idea. There's no telling who saw us."

"Who - or what," Chuck gulped. He stared at his uneaten PB&J. "My grandma says ghosts are real. She says her sister comes to visit her and tells her how her dead poodles are doing, and-"

"-No offense Chuck," Phil said, interrupting Chuck's ramble. "But your grandmother isn't exactly the most reliable source. Every expert worth knowing will tell you that instances of ghosts and paranormal phenomenon can be explained away by science or coincidence."

Germ smirked. "Who said anything about ghosts? Bill got scared by the wind. End of story."

"Are you serious?" Billy stared at him in disbelief. "First of all, you were just as scared as I was. Second, I'm not saying it was a ghost. But *someone* was watching us. And we still have no clue where the ball is."

"Maybe my estimate was off and it actually did get stuck in the shrubs or something," Phil said, shrugging.

Germ picked up a rogue straw and prepared a spitwad. "See Bill? No harm. No foul."

"Well if ghosts don't exist and it was just the wind, then we can go back and look for my ball... right?" Chuck asked, peering up meekly from his sandwich.

Germ choked on the spitwad. "*You?* Are you telling me 'Chicken Chuck' is going to strut right up to the Bryerwood House, knock on the front door and ask the Boogeyman for his ball back? The kid with a bunny night light?"

Chuck squirmed with embarrassment. Yes, he was still afraid of the dark. So much, that every night he made a mad dash from the lightswitch to bed, ensuring that no monsters or creepers could grab him before he made it to the safety of his covers. Once Germ had been by for a sleepover and witnessed this behavior firsthand, found it hilarious, and refused to let Chuck live it down.

Billy ignored Germ's attempts to deflect. "Chuck's right," he doubled down. "If you don't believe in ghosts then it shouldn't be any issue to go back, right *Jeremy*?"

Germ huffed. "You said yourself; it's trespassing, *William*. It's illegal."

The two friends glared at one another. A stalemate. You could cut the tension with a butter knife.

It was Germ who broke first. Gritting his teeth, he bent down to dig through his knapsack. From the front pocket he pulled a brand new baseball, and handed it to Chuck.

"Here. A replacement. Take it, and let's never speak of this again."

Chuck, beamed and pocketed the fresh ball. "Thanks Germ."

"Nothing to it."

The boys sat in awkward silence. Sure, Germ was a pain, but Billy was humbled by his gesture and felt bad for egging him on.

"Germ, I-"

"The part I can't shake," Germ interrupted. "Is the noise I heard. Coming from the house."

All eyes turned to him.

"Noise?" Phil asked, alarmed. "What noise?"

Billy was puzzled. "I don't remember any noise?"

"You sure about that?" Germ asked. "Maybe this will jog your memory." On cue, Germ let loose a loud and guttural *BELCH*.

The boys erupted with giggles, and Chuck laughed so hard that he snorted chocolate milk through his nostrils. With that one comedically timed burp, all was normal again. The dark cloud overhead lifted. Chatter ensued - homework, TV shows, and who would win in a fight between an alien and a mummy - and any inkling of strife or animosity was a distant memory.

CHAPTER 7

A Gift

And so, the weeks passed without much mention of the incident. Homework and after school activities piled up leaving less time for baseball, which the gang seemed fine with.

The weather cooled, the leaves turned, and fall was in midswing. Birds began the migration south to warmer winter climates. Jolly pumpkins adorned stoops, porches and windows, blissfully unaware of the plans to gut and carve them for decoration. Billy's father woke him up early on Saturdays to help rake the neverending cascade of leaves from the lawn. Things felt festive. The scent of the season was in both the air, and a wide selection of pastries.

Soon 'crept up like a black cat in the night, it was Halloween.

Billy could hardly contain his excitement when he woke up and checked the calendar. October 31st! Usually he stayed in bed until the very last minute reading comic books, but this morning he leapt up at the sound of his alarm, and even whistled on his way to the kitchen. When he got there, his dad was singing along to the radio while making breakfast, and raised an eyebrow at his son's equally chipper attitude.

"Heya, kiddo! You're in a good mood. Let me guess - stocks are up?"

Billy laughed and took a seat at the table. His dad worked in finance and liked to make cheesy jokes. Billy loved it.

"No dad! *Halloween!*"

"Ah, I see... then that would explain the sudden lull in mutual funds, and these... pumpkin pancakes!" Dramatically, his dad spun around to reveal a stack of pancakes etched with jack-o-lantern faces.

Billy grinned. "Stellar!"

"... Speaking of Halloween-" Billy's mom interjected, sashaying into the room. She was dressed in a sleek pantsuit.

"Big time lawyers need a big time breakfast," Billy's dad said, holding out a mug of coffee to her. She gave a kiss in return, then dropped down into the seat beside her son.

"Is everything good with Becca for tonight?" his mom asked. "Or do I need to call Jeremy's mother?"

Billy rolled his eyes discreetly enough that his mother wouldn't see, and sighed.

"Yes mom, everything's good."

This was a landmark Halloween. The first time the boys were allowed to go trick-or-treating on their own, without any parents. *Almost.*

Solo, save for the caveat that they be accompanied by Germ's older sister Becca, who, as he put it, was "a life-sucking Medusa, inflicting plague upon all who meet her."

Billy couldn't confirm the plague part, and Phil had to explain the Medusa reference which the other boys found fascinating. But if trick-or-treating with Becca was what it took not to be called babies at school the next day, it was worth it.

"Our hearing starts tomorrow so I've got to meet with counsel tonight. Your dad will be home to fix dinner, okay buddy?" Billy's mom ruffled his hair, then she grabbed her leather satchel and headed to the hall.

"Mom, but don't forget," he called after her as she opened the front door, "I need the finishing
touches for my costume."

"Perhaps I can be of service there?" Billy's dad struck a goofy pose, spatula in hand.

"You can sew?"

"I can... offer moral support."

Just then, Billy's mom hurried back into the kitchen, handing something to her son. As she rushed out, she called behind her. "You left this on the front porch - someone could've slipped on it and hurt themselves!"

Billy looked down at what his mother handed to him.

It was the Bryerwood House baseball.

CHAPTER 8

Dr. Jekyll

Billy stared at the clock above the classroom door. He was in English, the period right before lunch, and counting down the seconds until he could meet the guys. The morning had been a blur. He got to school early, biking twice the normal speed, and left a note scribbled "URGENT" in Germ's locker, instructing him to assemble the crew for an emergency lunch meeting. Phil had science club during lunch on Thursdays and wasn't going to like it, but Billy was confident that the dire nature of the situation preempted a young boy's thirst for knowledge and discovery.

Usually English was one of Billy's favorite classes. He liked to read, plus his teacher, Mr. Reinholdt, was a pretty cool guy. When Billy told him that the school librarian said his *Heroic Adventures of Seagull Man* comic wasn't a "real book," Mr. Reinholdt said that even though comics don't resemble books in the traditional sense, they still deliver important and well-told stories. Mr. Reinholdt even revealed that he himself was a proud collector!

Mr. Reinholdt was also a teacher known for his interesting lesson plans, and today was no exception; for the past month, the class had been covering monsters in literature. Nevertheless, Billy just couldn't concentrate and found his thoughts drifting.

Pacing at the chalkboard, Mr. Reinholdt brandished a well-worn copy of *Strange Case of Dr. Jekyll and Mr. Hyde* by Robert Louis Stevenson, last week's assigned reading.

"You're probably asking yourself 'why does Dr Jekyll create Mr. Hyde in the first place?' 'How can a person be drawn to do something so drastic?'" Mr Reinholdt paused, letting this sink in for dramatic emphasis. "Jekyll creates Hyde so he can embrace his darkest, secret desires. And it isn't until the line between the two men blurs beyond recognition and Jekyll can no longer control Hyde, that he sees the error of his ways.

"So. What message do you think Robert Louis Stevenson was trying to convey to the reader?" Mr. Reinholdt folded his arms and scanned the room. "Let's hear from... Billy."

Billy was so distracted, contemplating the surprise package from this morning, that he wasn't prepared for Mr. Reinholdt's question.

"Well..." he took a deep breath, stalling for time. "I think... maybe he was trying to say... that if Jekyll had just..." Billy struggled. "Well, if he had made a different potion... because Hyde wasn't..."

It was no use. Billy didn't know the answer. He could feel his face boiling hot, turning crimson. Mr. Reinholdt's brow was furrowed and he looked ready to reprimand Billy, until a steady voice from the back of the room spoke.

"Perhaps," the voice interjected, "he was saying that there wasn't a real line in the first place."

Mr. Reinholdt craned his neck. "Vanessa? Is that you? Please, go on."

Billy swiveled in his seat, and locked eyes with Vanessa De-lille. She was a recent transfer to their school, though no one knew much about her. She and Germ shared a PE class and he'd christened her a "first class weirdo." Billy wasn't sure about the weirdo part, but she was definitely unusual, and fairly aloof. Quiet, kept to herself, and unlike the other girls in their grade who favored neon and ruffles, wore a lot of black clothes that were fairly threadbare and old.

"Jekyll took the serum so he could do terrible things without recourse, pinning the responsibility to someone he saw as separate from himself. That way, Hyde could be the bad guy, and Jekyll could live without guilt. But isn't Jekyll just as bad for enabling Hyde's behavior? For creating a scapegoat, a conduit, so that his deepest monstrosities could be realized? It raises the question as to whether there's any duality between these two men. Or if they're one and the same."

Vanessa finished speaking and clasped her hands together on her desk. By this point, every kid in the class was turned and gawking at her. Mr. Reinholdt stood with his mouth slightly agape, but caught himself and quickly recovered.

"Or maybe," Vanessa continued. "Maybe it was just an accident. Jekyll went too far. Simple as that. End of story."

With that, she disengaged from the discussion and began to write furiously in her notebook, seemingly oblivious to the impact she'd made on her peers.

Suddenly the bell rang, signaling the end of the class. The other students were jolted from their trance and hastily grabbed their belongings, filing out.

"Be careful, tonight!" Mr. Reinholdt called after them as he wiped off the chalkboard. "All sorts of ghoulish happenings transpire on 'All Hallows Eve.' And if you come across Mr. Hyde... maybe try trick-or-treating at another house?"

He gave a grin, then, calling over his shoulder, added, "oh, and Billy. Hang back a second."

Billy had been mid-step out the door, hightailing it to meet his friends in the cafeteria. Halting abruptly, he backtracked to Mr. Reinholdt's desk.

"You seemed out of it today. Everything okay?" Mr. Reinholdt looked concerned.

Hesitating a moment, Billy went for it. "Mr. Reinholdt, do you believe in ghosts? Or real monsters?" This wasn't a question he'd pose to most adults, but his teacher was different.

Pausing in thought, Mr. Reinholdt set down the chalkboard brush.

"During the day? No. But I believe when you cast enough darkness, and enough doubt, ghosts and monsters can be made of us all."

Billy looked back, confused. "I don't think I entirely understand that, but thanks."

Mr. Reinholdt smiled. "All the better that you don't. Anyway, try to focus in class the rest of the day, okay?"

Billy nodded, taking this as a cue that he was free to leave. Scooping up his book bag he made for the door, breaking into a run and almost colliding with Vanessa, who was standing outside the classroom.

She was jotting something down in her notebook, seemingly unaware that she was blocking the flow of foot traffic. Billy skidded around her. He shook his head, dismayed. It wasn't until he was halfway down the hall that she finally looked up.

"First class weirdo, alright," Billy muttered to himself.

Vanessa Delile watched with piqued interest as Billy ran to meet his friends.

CHAPTER 9

Emergency Meeting

"**I**t's the same ball." Phil squinted, his eyeball an inch from the worn leather laces. "Look, at the writing." Sure enough, CHUCK was hurriedly scrawled on it in permanent marker.

"Holy smokes, that's it!" Chuck exclaimed. He held the ball up like it was a long lost treasure found in a recently unearthed crypt.

Germ gritted his teeth. "Bill, if you're pulling some kind of prank, that's my department."

"You were there with me that day," Billy said, "you know I wouldn't joke about this."

Phil set the ball down in the center of the table. The boys sat in awe for a moment. Eventually it was Germ who broke the silence.

"Okay. I'll bite. Let's say it *is* the ball. How?"

"Maybe it didn't actually land in the Bryerwood yard like we thought," Chuck chimed in, spitting the words through a mouthful of mac and cheese. "Maybe the house next door?"

Phil shook his head adamantly. "It was a big swing, but not that big. Chuck, is there any chance your brother's messing with us?"

"I mean... there's *always* a chance of that," Chuck gave a grim smile. "But how would he know about us losing the ball in the first place? He couldn't. He was at the park"

"So that means..." Billy slowly connected the dots. "...That someone else was there. Someone saw us and knew where to bring the ball. They knew where I lived"

"But Chuck and I kept watch on the street, there was no one around," Phil protested.

Billy swallowed hard. "If you didn't see anyone in the street, it means it had to come from..." he trailed off, his mind swirling with dark possibilities. "The house. Inside. Someone was *watching* us. Whoever it was that slammed the door shut."

Germ threw his sandwich down on the table, causing some lettuce to fly out from between the bread slices. "Stop making stuff up, Bill. That house is empty! The wind blew the door shut. And look, you're scaring Chuck."

They all turned to Chuck who was wide-eyed, biting his lip.

"I'm not scared!" he snorted, despite most definitely being scared. "But... but what if Billy's right? Or even worse. What if all the stories about Bryerwood House are true? And a GHOST brought the ball to your porch?!"

"How would a ghost know where I live?" Billy asked, staring at Chuck incredulously.

"Ghosts know everything," Chuck replied, sagely.

"Oh please," Germ rolled his eyes. "Watch this." Scrambling onto his chair, he climbed and stood on the lunch table. Then, putting two fingers in his mouth, he let loose a loud WHISTLE, causing all cafeteria chatter to come to a standstill.

"What are you doing?" Billy hissed. He swiveled around in his seat to see all the other kids looking at them as if they were aliens who had crash-landed from outer space.

Germ puffed out his chest and projected to the room. "Who here believes in ghosts?"

There was a silence. No reaction. Some whispers. One kid in the back of the lunchroom faintly yelled at Germ to "sit down," and it got a few laughs.

Billy sighed. Against his better judgement, he joined Germ atop the table.

"Who here," Billy called out, "thinks that Bryerwood House is haunted?"

Another silence, this time broken by an overwhelming number of hands rising into the air, and murmurings of "yes" and "duh" throughout the room.

Billy raised an eyebrow at Germ, who shrugged, rolled his eyes again, then sat down accepting his defeat.

Before Billy returned to his seat, he caught the eye of Vanessa. She stood alone at the opposite end of the cafeteria, leaned against the wall beneath a cobwebbed banner that read "Happy Halloween." Her arms were crossed and her gaze bore into Billy. He gulped. Weirdo.

Germ looked exasperated, but that was the norm for him. Taking a bite of his apple, he recovered. "Okay, okay. At the very least we've deduced that a bunch of babies - and liars - go to this school. But I'll admit; something's up. I won't say it's a ghost, but there's a stink in the air."

Chuck grimaced and clutched at his stomach. "Sorry, that's me. Mac and cheese." He shrugged apologetically.

"No Chuck, that's not what he means," Billy laughed. "But you're right, Germ. Something's up. That's for sure."

CHAPTER 10

Danger Kevin

That evening, as promised, Billy's dad had his costume ready; a replica Danger Kevin ensemble, Billy's all-time favorite TV stuntman. Danger Kevin rode a souped-up motorcycle and performed death-defying feats to wow the crowd. Basically every kid's hero.

Billy's mom made the jumpsuit and his dad spray painted an old motorcycle helmet with a stenciled insignia. But, the *pièce de résistance* was an officially licensed Danger Kevin cape which Billy had saved for by doing chores (and his parents generously paid the rest).

After school that day, Billy, Germ, Phil and Chuck made arrangements to meet at Billy's house since the candy haul in Billy and Phil's neighborhood was particularly generous. Before the other boys arrived, Billy and his dad ate some lasagna, another of his dad's culinary specialties. After dinner Billy suited up, then he and his dad dug around in the shed for spare materials - old tires, particle board, rope - to create a makeshift stunt course in the backyard. It was a lot of fun and took "Danger Billy's" mind off the mysterious reappearing baseball.

The first to show up was Phil. He was dressed in a hooded robe that looked like something out of the Renaissance, and carried a weathered scroll under his arm.

Billy stared at his friend blankly. "What are you supposed to be?"

"Guess!" Phil said, unraveling the scroll and striking a pose.

"Uh... a monk?"

"Nope."

"Err..." Billy looked from the scroll to the feathered quill in Phil's hand. "Shakespeare?"

"No, but getting closer. I'm indeed someone with a classically brilliant mind."

Crickets. Billy was dumbfounded.

Phil sighed. "I'm Italian mathematician and cosmological theorist Giordano Bruno."

Billy's dad nodded emphatically. "Of course! I see it now." As soon as Phil turned away to stow his scroll, Mr. Marsden gave Billy a confused shrug.

Phil joined in the stunt course fun for a bit, but his robe kept getting stuck in the spokes of Billy's bike. A short time later the doorbell rang signaling Chuck's arrival. He waddled through the front door, his face bright red.

Though he requested to be "one of the chipmunks, preferably Alvin," this was misinterpreted by his grandmother as simply "a chipmunk." A miscommunication caught too late, leaving Chuck with no alternative. And so, he was clad head-to-toe in shaggy brown fur, accessorized with matching ears and a painted black nose.

Chuck looked on enviously at Billy's Danger Kevin costume.

Billy noticed and insisted that his friend try the cape on over his furry bodysuit, causing the three boys to erupt with giggles at the newly christened character of "Danger Munk," a chipmunk with a penchant for the extreme.

Germ made a bombastic entrance, as always, decked out in a black pinstripe suit, fedora, and armed with a Tommy Gun tucked unfastidiously in his pumpkin shaped candy carrier. A confident glint in his eye, he strutted through the doorway, then swiftly drew the gun, raising one eyebrow.

"Gimme all your candy or you'll be sleepin' with the fishes!"

Billy's dad rushed into the hall from the kitchen, pointing a banana.

"Looks like we got ourselves a good ol' fashioned shootout." Germ and Billy's dad fired off a slew of imaginary rounds at one another, with the appropriate "pew-pew!" sound effects accompanying. Eventually Billy's dad took a pretend bullet to the shoulder and begged for mercy. Before Germ could exact swift justice, the door swung open with gusto. On the other side was Becca, Germ's older sister, who charged right in.

"Jeremy, tell your friends that I-" Becca caught herself, taking stock of Billy's dad, keeled over on the floor.

"Hi Mr. Marsden."

Billy's dad gave a wave, still clutching at his imaginary wound.

"Heya kiddo!"

Dressed in a lace dress, elbow-length gloves, layers of pearls, and armed with a glittering microphone, Becca was doing her best imitation of a pop singer. Ever the charming younger brother, Germ had egged her on during the car ride over, comparing her outlandishly crimped hair to that of a groomed poodle.

Their relationship was strained as ever.

Becca popped a bubble with her gum, crossed her arms and glared down at Germ. "Jeremy, tell your friends that *I'm in charge*, and they better be ready to leave once Margie gets here."

"Who's Margie?" Billy asked.

Germ rolled his eyes. "Her dumb friend Margie's coming with us." Germ dodged an elbow from Becca. "Margie's sister's in our Civics class... Sarah Vasquez. You know, the one that tripped off stage and landed on her face during the holiday assembly last year? She's coming too. *Apparently.*"

Becca swatted at Germ. "Don't you dare bring that up, you little dweeb! Margie says Sarah's very sensitive about it; she had to have full nasal reconstructive surgery."

Chuck leaned over to Billy. "If you ask me, her face looks better now," he whispered.

On cue, the doorbell rang and Becca gave Germ a stern "don't you dare" kind of look. Billy opened the door to find Margie standing on the porch, clad in hot pink aerobics gear, with the name "BARBIE" splashed across her shirt. She squealed and beelined for Becca. They clutched one another in the type of hug reserved for only teen girls and soldiers returning to their families after a long stint overseas.

Behind Margie stood two figures dressed in long black dresses, pointed black hats, and draped with shawls. Witches. One, Billy recognized, as the aforementioned Sarah Vasquez, who, in addition to a couple of warts plastered to her face, also had a fake crooked nose concealing her real one.

Probably for the best, Billy thought to himself, recalling how Sarah fell face-first into an oversized tuba.

Standing next to Sarah was someone who Billy was shocked

to see on his doorstep, of all places. Someone he couldn't seem to avoid today; Vanessa Delile.

"Can we come in?" she asked, flatly.

"We have to be invited," chimed in Sarah. "It's the rule."

Vanessa sighed. "That's vampires. He's just blocking the doorway."

Billy stumbled back, mumbling "sorry" and let the girls pass. Huddling to the side of the room. Germ, Phil and Chuck stood rigid, mouths agape. None had ever been in such close quarters to so many girls outside of school.

"Great costumes, girls!" Billy's dad exclaimed.

"Thanks Mr. Marsden!" they replied in unison.

Sarah pulled a face and pointed one long, fake, black fingernail at the boys. "I'll get you, my pretties!"

The boys reflexively flinched. Flourishing her hands as if conjuring a spell, Sarah lunged toward Chuck.

"And your little dog too!"

Chuck, utterly flustered, recoiled, almost losing his footing. "I-I-I'm a chipmunk!" he stammered.

Becca clapped her hands together, sending spray-on glitter flying in all directions. "Alright everyone, time to go... Lots of trick-or-treating to be had!" She ushered Germ and the boys toward the door, and gestured to Margie to do the same with Vanessa and Sarah.

"This will either be excellent... or really, really bad," Phil whispered to his friends on their way out.

"Don't even get me started," Germ replied.

"Have fun, gang!" Billy's dad waved as the kids embarked on their Halloween adventure, and shut the door with a flourish. Then, a glint in his eye, he dipped a hand into the candy cauldron posted by the door, procuring a gooey mini caramel. If he wasn't chaperoning the kids this year it was only fair that Dad get dibs on the family stash.

CHAPTER 11

Trick-or-Treat

T he night started off fairly smooth and without incident. Becca and Margie kept fifteen paces behind the younger kids, giggling and gossiping about the dramatic dealings of their inner social circle. When Germ asked why the girls hung back and didn't go get candy, Becca tossed her hair over her shoulder and proclaimed that candy was "kid's stuff."

There was an obvious division between the boys and younger girls at first. Billy, Phil, Chuck and Germ weren't sure how to talk to Vanessa and Sarah, or if they even *wanted* to talk to them. But the awkward silences ended when Phil challenged Chuck to blow a bubble with the full force of six sticks of gum, and, instead of creating a bubble, the gum coagulated into a giant goopy wad that Chuck spit across the sidewalk with one strained blow. The kids all erupted into laughter and giggles. From that point onward the ice was broken, and an intricate system of candy trading was underway, along with a friendly rivalry to see who could collect the most before night's end.

At one point Billy stopped to re-lace his boots and Vanessa fell behind next to him. They walked in silence for what seemed like an eternity to Billy, until Vanessa spoke up.

"You're in my English class," she said. Whether it was a statement or a question, Billy didn't know.

"Uh... yeah."

"You're the *Jekyll and Hyde* guy."

Billy cleared his throat. "You know, I was getting around to answering that question by the way-"

"This year?" Vanessa smirked as she said it and Billy blushed. "I'm kidding."

As strange as she was, Billy liked Vanessa's wry sense of humor. He gave an awkward grin then changed the subject.

"So you and Sarah are good friends? I didn't know that."

"Friends? No, not really. Her mom volunteered on our field trip last week and noticed I was new, so she forced Sarah to invite me out tonight. But Sarah's not all bad. In fact, we're starting a coven."

"A 'coven?'"

"Family of witches," Vanessa replied, matter-of-factly. "Dark sisterhood. Peak feminism." She paused. "And we can cast spells and stuff."

"Like magic?" Billy looked at her, incredulously. Vanessa didn't confirm nor deny, instead dramatically tossing her long braid over one shoulder.

"How do you know so much about that kind of stuff?" Billy asked.

Vanessa eyed him. "What... kind of 'stuff'?"

"Like monsters and spells and..." Billy trailed off.

"You mean the occult? The macabre?"

"Yeah, I guess."

Vanessa stopped in her tracks. On her face she wore an amused expression. Almost like she was... happy? Up to this point Vanessa behaved fairly detached and subdued, but this was the first time Billy saw her display any level of excitement.

"Do you ever wonder about the forces unseen? The things that go bump in the night?" Vanessa's eyes gleamed as she asked.

"I try not to think about that stuff," Billy replied, reflecting back on his sleepless nightmare-filled nights that followed the incident at Bryerwood House.

"Most people don't. It's easier that way." As Vanessa spoke, she stared intensely at Billy, emptying a packet of Pop Rocks into her mouth. Billy considered telling Vanessa what happened at Bryerwood. It seemed like something she would be into. But by that point the two had caught up with the rest of the group, and consequently their conversation cut short.

Sarah was competing with Chuck to see who could make the funniest chipmunk face (Chuck, with a natural advantage, was winning), while Phil and Germ played judge.

"A sour pop goes to whoever does the best chirp," Germ dangled the candy high like a carrot before a prize pony.

"Get a load of this!" Chuck pursed his lips, jutting out his two front teeth, and brought his hands curled in under his chin, like paws. The other kids laughed, but were interrupted by Becca who strode to the front of the group and clapped for everyone's attention.

"Listen up! Margie and I are going to meet some friends. Alone. You kids stay in a six block radius, don't get into trouble, and meet us back here at ten o'clock sharp. Got it?"

Taken aback, the younger kids exchanged worried looks. All except Germ, who threw his hands up, exasperated.

"What! No way, we've already hit up most of these houses! And mom told you to stay with us."

"As if I care, Jeremy," Becca rolled her eyes. "You're lucky we stayed with you this long." She twirled a piece of crimped hair on her finger. Meanwhile, Sarah and her older sister Margie broke-off from the group, engaged in their own tense whisper.

"Maybe we should just go home," Phil said, tugging at his robes which had been dragging all night.

"Yeah," chimed in Billy. "My dad will be upset if he thinks we're out here alone."

"No, no... it's Halloween, you have to stay out and have fun!" Becca's cool act wavered momentarily, and there was a touch of desperation in her voice. Germ smiled devilishly.

"Ah, I see what's happening here; all the little dots are connecting." His sordid expression matched his skeezy mobster costume. "The Beckster's technically grounded. Mom found a lipstick she stole from the mall department store." He shook his head in mock disapproval. "Yeah, I didn't want to believe it either. Teens these days - the trouble they get into."

Becca shot Germ a filthy glare. He continued with his examination.

"Young Becca here *needs* us to stay out. If I go home and she's not with me, my mom will know. Then, the jig is up."

"Fine, you little brat," Becca hissed, practically spitting venom at her younger brother. "What do you want?

"Your Gameboy. For a week,' said Germ, without hesitation.

"As if! No. No way."

Germ clasped his hands in a tent and stared back at his sister, stoically. "These are my terms."

Becca glared at him, seething in silence. It was apparent to the other boys that Germ was loving every second of this, knowing that he had the upper hand on his older sister, and could play puppetmaster to her fate.

After some tense deliberation, Becca let out a defeated sigh. "Ugh. Fine. A week, but you don't get any of my games."

Germ pumped his fist in victory. "Deal. Your games suck anyway." He spun around to face the other kids who were looking back, unsure if they'd gotten the raw deal out of the arrangement or not.

"C'mon guys! It'll be fun!"

CHAPTER 12

Breaking the Rules

Becca and Margie left, excitedly chattering about their plans to meet the other sophomores at Lookout Point, the place where all the cool teenage kids hung out. Meanwhile, Germ rallied his troops.

"All right. Who wants to go to Maple Road?" he asked, rubbing his hands together, a mischievous smile on his face.

Phil shook his head. "That's outside of the six block radius, dude."

"So what?"

Sarah frowned, picking at a shoddily glued wart. "Margie said if we go far we'll get into trouble and that means she'll get into trouble, and then my life will be a living hell."

"Whatever," said Germ. "Margie chose this life when she decided to befriend that she-devil." Deal or no deal, there was no love lost between Germ and his sister. He turned to Billy.

"Come on, Bill. They'll listen to you. *Please.* Let's go to Maple Road. You and I both know those houses give out the best candy. FULL SIZE BARS." His eyes shone in the streetlights. "We get the goods, then head straight back here."

Billy looked into Germ's eyes, reading his desperation, then turned to survey the faces of his friends. Phil's expression was pleading; *don't do it.* Chuck was distracted, digging through his candy sack. Sarah, still frowning, shook her head while anxiously tapping her foot.

But Vanessa. Vanessa had a twinkle in her eye. Her gaze bore into Billy's. She wasn't worried about trouble, or parents, or what might be out there in the night. Her face bore the expression of genuine curiosity.

"I suppose... we could go to Maple Road, do a quick lap, then come straight back," Billy said, caving.

Germ cheered and broke into a happy march, racing toward Maple Road without a look back. Vanessa gave Billy a smirk and followed, with Chuck behind and Sarah in tow. Giving a defeated shrug, Phil joined the procession, struggling to walk without stepping on the hem of his oversized robe.

Straightening his Danger Kevin cape, Billy brought up the rear, wondering why he always gave into Germ's wild schemes.

CHAPTER 13

Back to Bryerwood

T he gang got to Maple Road without incident. To Germ's delight, all that he promised was true.

Sure enough - and at the very first house no less - a little old lady in a shawl made of prop spiderwebs was handing out full-size candy bars. Chuck's eyes lit up. This was his Valhalla. With renewed vigor, the kids quickened their pace and made for the next house.

Ding dong. The door swung open with gusto. Standing with her hands on her hips was Mrs. Phelps, P.E. teacher and coach of just about every team at school. A formidable woman, Mrs. Phelps was built like a line-backer and with a life-size personality to match. Even in her downtime she was wearing a tracksuit, albeit this one was at least holiday themed, a stretched pumpkin pattern. Nevertheless, Billy couldn't quite account for why she had a whistle hanging around her neck at this time of night.

"Heya kids!" Mrs. Phelps bellowed.

"Trick-or-treat!" the group replied in unison, raising their voices to be heard over the sound of a football game blaring at max volume on the television three rooms away.

Mrs. Phelps plunged a meaty hand into her candy bucket, retrieving generous handfuls which she deposited into each outstretched sack. "Gotta fatten you shrinky dinks up!"

The kids' eyes lit up at the sight of the portions. All except Germ who, unserved, held out his hand expectantly. Mrs. Phelps eyed him. Then, half-heartedly, she handed over a single piece of candy which fell into Germ's bag with a pathetic *plop.*

"One?!" he exclaimed, indignantly.

"I haven't forgotten about that healthy dose of sour cream *someone* added to my protein shake last week!" Before closing the door, Mrs. Phelps scowled and clutched at her stomach as if reliving past indigestion. A steamed Germ gave a half-hearted kick at her porch banister in defiance as the other kids burst out laughing at his comeuppance.

From there on they tackled the neighborhood with the swiftness of a military raid. With each house the candy sacks and pails grew fuller and the mood lightened. A rising feeling of invincibility, steeled by this newfound sugary wealth. It was a downright candy haul! Plus, everyone was having a great time.

Caught up in excited chatter, the group absent-mindedly rounded a corner, turning onto a small cul-de-sac. Much less populated with trick-or-treaters than the surrounding neighborhood streets. And for good reason. At the top of the dead-end stood Bryerwood House, looking particularly eerie on this Hallow's Eve. The sight prompted the four boys to stop dead in their tracks. Phil was caught so off-guard that his candy bag spilled over.

"We should head back," Billy said, looking around nervously. He glanced over at Chuck who was clutching his chipmunk ears and shaking his head fervently.

"Why?" Vanessa asked.

Billy didn't have a good answer. "It's... getting late."

Vanessa regarded him, puzzled. "Fine. But let's do these houses, we have plenty of time. Then we'll loop back around."

"No." Germ stepped forward, brandishing his toy BB gun as he spoke. "Bill's right. We've gone too far. Gotta head back to meet the sinister sisters."

"What?" Vanessa exclaimed. "This was *your* idea."

The boys exchanged uneasy looks.

"We have plenty of time," Sarah chimed in. "Like Vanessa said, we can go to these houses," she gestured to the cul-de-sac, "then loop around AND do the other side on our way back, I don't understa-"

A realization dawned over her, and her gaze shifted to the house at the end of the street.

"Ooh..." Sarah's mouth transformed into a smirk. "You're *scared* of the Bryerwood House."

Billy's face flushed red, the color of his Danger Kevin helmet. Chuck stared at his paws while Phil tugged nervously at his robes. Germ brushed it off.

"Yeah, right," he laughed, anxiously. "Scared of what, exactly?"

"I used to be scared of it when I was little," Sarah shrugged. "It's understandable."

"We're not *scared*," Germ puffed his chest out. Billy noticed Germ was avoiding eye contact with him.

"Yeah!" Chuck exclaimed. "You think we're scared? Pfft. Well... we're not." Chuck mirrored Germ's stance and the two gave their best impression of bravery.

Sarah folded her arms, raising one skeptical eyebrow. "Okay. Then go to the Bryerwood House. Knock on the door and trick-or-treat."

This left Germ speechless. He could do nothing but stare back at Sarah, who, armed with the upperhand, was prepared for a stand-off. Luckily, Germ was spared by Vanessa.

"I'll do it." She had walked closer to Bryerwood, and now stood in the center of the cul-de-sac, bathed in the full moonlight. The house loomed behind her like a dark colossus.

"Do what?" Billy asked, incredulously.

"Go trick-or-treat there." Vanessa's face was blank, expressionless, a complete contrast to Chuck whose eyes were wide.

"Are you crazy?!" He flung his arms out, exasperated, causing his chipmunk paws to fly off his hands (luckily they were safety-pinned to his sleeves).

"What?" She stared back. "It's just a house."

They all stood, aghast. Even Sarah, who had so brazenly questioned Germ.

"Vanessa, I was just joking. Teasing the guys," she stammered.

"No one trick-or-treats at Bryerwood House. It's unheard of," said Phil.

"Why?" Vanessa asked, and Billy searched desperately for an answer. "Ghosts," he half-whispered, the best he could come up with.

"*Ghosts*? And you have evidence of these ghosts?"

"Look sister, you don't *need* evidence when everyone knows it," Germ stepped forward, arms crossed. "You're new, I get it. But there isn't a kid around here who doesn't know that Bryerwood House is bad news. No one touches it with a ten foot pole. You haven't heard the stories-"

"-Let me guess," Vanessa interrupted, crossing her arms to mirror Germ's. "A monster, locked in the basement? The ghost of a widow, haunting the attic? Demonic dolls that come to life? The Boogeyman, lurking in the shadows..."

"... How do you know?" Chuck stared at her in astonishment.

"I know, because I *know*. There's always a house, and there's always a group of kids, making up stories to scare one another. Not giving a second thought."

The boys eyed one another. Billy was starting to feel a bit sheepish and judging by the looks on his friends' faces, they felt the same.

"So I'm going to go there and trick-or-treat." Vanessa said, her voice firm.

Billy made one last attempt to stop her. "But trick-or-treat with who? No one even lives there."

"Then why is the light on?"

Silently raising one hand, Vanessa pointed up at the house. Sure enough, in the highest window, a light was on. The boys stared, mouths agape. *How was this possible?*

Before anyone could react, Vanessa was already striding through the gates of Bryerwood House in a beeline to the front porch. Quickly enveloped by the darkness.

CHAPTER 14

Noogie Nick

"I knew she was weird, but this is downright cuckoo." Germ paced back-and-forth, wringing his pinstripe fedora in his hands. "She's gonna give Chuck a damn heart-attack"

Chuck was hunched on the curb, wiping sweat from his brow. The chipmunk costume was very unforgiving, especially in distressing times like these.

"Why didn't I wear any underwear beneath this thing?" he lamented.

"Ew, gross," Sarah grimaced. "And chill out, okay? I know it's creepy, but Vanessa's right. It's just a house."

Even so, Billy couldn't help but obsessively check his watch (a hand-me-down Timex of his dad's which he'd been pretty proud to receive). A minute and thirteen seconds had passed since Vanessa had gone inside the Bryerwood lot, more than enough time to grab a handful of candy and be back.

"Look," Billy sighed. "Sarah, you might as well know. There was... an incident."

Phil's eyes grew wide. Germ shook his head and drew his index finger across his throat.

"What kind of *incident*?" she asked.

"We were playing baseball. Except we couldn't go to the park so we had to find somewhere else to play. And-"

Before Billy could continue, he was cut-off by a snickering, vitriol-laden voice, coming from down the street.

"Well, well, well. If it isn't the pansy squad!"

It was Noogie Nick, Chuck's notoriously evil older brother, who was approaching fast on a BMX bike. One of his friends - the zit-faced and aptly nicknamed "Slug" - took a swing at a smaller kid passing by, knocking the kid's candy bucket to the ground. The bullies cackled and cheered at this pathetic "victory." Slug did a loop and scooped up a handful of fallen candy, scarfing it back behind pimpled lips.

"What do we do?!" Chuck half-whispered in terror.

Phil stared at him in astonishment. "Are you serious, Chuck? He's YOUR brother!"

Noogie Nick skidded his bike to a stop in front of the boys. Billy gulped and scanned the area looking for a quick exit strategy. It was no use. Nick was flanked by his cronies and had them surrounded on almost all sides.

Nick, Slug, and Metal Mike were the toughest, meanest kids in the neighborhood, and they looked the part. Mike earned his moniker due to the metal plate he had in his elbow, the product of a dirt bike accident. A month in the hospital and several broken bones later, Mike was lucky that this was the worst of his injuries, given that he also wasn't wearing a helmet. Even so, some kids swore that prior to the accident Mike had been an honor roll student. Hard to believe, as Metal Mike was mid-way through his third attempt at the eleventh grade. Low IQ or not, Metal Mike was mean, dumb, and threw that elbow around like a concealed weapon.

Slug was a different story. One of those kids who looked like he hadn't seen a shower in weeks. Greasy and acne-ridden, he hid behind stringy, unwashed hair. The kind of kid whose mom bought him new clothes yet he insisted on cycling through the same three dirty, ragged t-shirts. When Slug was on his own (sans Nick) he wasn't a bully, but he did vandalize other kids' property, tagging their bikes and book bags with crusty old spray paint.

Even at their worst, Slug and Metal Mike were nothing compared to the terror that was Noogie Nick.

It's unclear what made Nick so bad; if he was born that way, or something happened to him. Though a few years younger, Chuck recalls them sharing similar childhood experiences, albeit Nick gravitated toward "different interests." *Darker* interests. Like trying to kill squirrels and other small animals with his slingshot. Stuff that serial killers do as kids. Nick derived pure pleasure from the suffering of those weaker than him. He was rotten to the very core, and it was a genetic joke that he and Chuck shared the same DNA. Nick terrorized his little brother for sport and Chuck never once fought back.

"H-h-hi Nick," Chuck stammered. "You didn't t-tell me you were trick-or-treating tonight."

Nick laughed, but the sound of it sent shivers down Billy's spine. A malicious, downright mean cackle. "Trick-or-treating is for babies and idiots. Do I look like a baby or an idiot, snot-face?"

Chuck's face turned bright red. "N-no."

Metal Mike rounded on Germ, snatched his fedora and put it on. "Look, I'm Al Calzone!" The other bullies guffawed as Mike put his hand up to the side of Germ's head, shaped his fingers into a gun, and mock-fired. Then he took the hat off and flung it to the ground.

"Haha, good one, Mike," Germ chirped, chuckling nervously.

"I believe the name you're looking for is that of the gangster 'Al Capone,'" corrected Phil.

The bullies turned and wordlessly stared at Phil. Slug spit on the ground and Billy could smell his rank saliva from three feet away. Nick's eyes narrowed. He cracked his knuckles and walked up to Phil.

"You think you're so smart, huh nerd?" Noogie Nick taunted. He yanked Phil's candy bag from him and began rifling through it.

"Garbage, garbage... I'll take it... sucks... take it.... garbage," Nick pocketed the select pieces and dumped the rest of the bag out onto the concrete. Phil's face was white as a ghost.

"That's..." he began.

"*That's what,* nerd?" Nick jeered. "I'll put this in terms you'll understand. Do the math; you, a big nerd minus your candy, equals a big nerd, dumb, baby, *loser.*"

Nick's cronies laughed at his pathetic excuse for humor. Phil's lower lip quivered, and he blinked rapidly, fighting back tears. *Enough is enough*, thought Billy.

"Hey!" he cried out. Stepping boldly forward, Billy felt as if he was watching himself from above, like an out-of-body experience. "That's Phil's candy! You pick it up and give it back to him. *Or else.*"

Chuck gasped, and Germ's expression oscillated between terrified and impressed. Sarah, who had been watching silently on the outskirts of the skirmish, turned on her heel, and ran.

"Tell Vanessa I'll see her tomorrow!" she called behind her, without looking back.

Billy knew he had crossed a line with Nick, but he wasn't going to let anyone talk to his friends like that. Which didn't mean that he wasn't scared out of his mind, because he WAS, extremely. Regardless, he couldn't stand silently by and allow this ugly, low-brained thug to further harass them.

Noogie Nick cracked his knuckles. Metal Mike slapped his elbow, causing a *ping* sound to emanate. Slug pulled a rusty can of spray paint from his back jean pocket.

"Or else what?" Nick growled again.

"Or else..." Billy was sweating, even though the night air was growing chiller. "Or else... RUN!"

And that's when all hell broke loose. Scrambling, the boys desperately tried to evade the bullies, and escape the cul-de-sac.

Billy and Phil darted to the right only to be cut-off by Mike who gave an exaggerated swing of his elbow. Fortunately for them, he missed. Germ and Chuck dodged to the left, getting stopped in their tracks by Slug who let loose his spray can, catching the tip of Chuck's chipmunk tail.

Noogie Nick and his goons had the boys cornered without escape; Mike on the right, Slug on the left, Nick front and center. Behind the boys stood Bryerwood House. Like hyenas circling their prey, the bullies closed in. Illuminated by the flickering lights of neighborhood jack-o-lanterns, Nick looked especially demonic. From his pocket, he brandished a metal chain. "Nowhere to run," he snarled.

The four boys clutched one another, terrified. As afraid as he was, Billy knew what they had to do.

"That's where you're wrong, Nick!" He shouted. "Come on, guys!"

Turning tail, Billy broke into a sprint, his friends following suit. They ran at full speed taking the only escape route available, behind them, straight into the yard of Bryerwood House.

Noogie Nick, Metal Mike and Slug stopped in their tracks. Billy's hunch had been correct; for all their bluster, Nick and his friends wouldn't go anywhere near the Bryerwood House, even if their reputations depended on it. Bullies are, more often than not, the biggest cowards of all.

CHAPTER 15

Looking for Vanessa

B illy and the boys ran so fast that their remaining candy fell and scattered, disappearing forever in the tall grass. Let it fall, Billy thought. He and his friends dashed through a thicket of dense brush and trees, dodging fallen branches and cracked stone walkway. Before realizing it, they were running up the steps of Bryerwood's rickety old porch, leaping two at a time. Just ahead loomed the ominous front door, once again wide open like a hinged jaw, exposing the dark recesses within.

Except now it looked strangely... *inviting*. Billy couldn't explain it. He and the other boys felt drawn inside, as if some invisible force was pulling them despite their better judgement and fear. Quite inexplicably hypnotic. It was because of this magnetic attraction that, without looking back, the boys ran right through and into the unknown.

Threshold crossed, the door swung shut with an echoing *SLAM*, followed by nothing but darkness. Without hesitation, the house claimed its prey.

Billy felt disoriented and in a daze, and bent over to catch his breath. Squinting, he peered into the low light. "Are you guys all right?" he asked. Little by little his vision adjusted and his friends materialized.

"I'm... okay..." Chuck wheezed, managing a weak smile. Germ scowled and gave a thumbs-up.

"Me too," Phil said, nodding between gasps, his asthma at risk of triggering. "But there's no way of knowing if Nick and his goons are still out there. Waiting." Having torn the bottom of his costume running through a thorny patch in the yard, Phil said this as he hastily fashioned the loose ends into a makeshift hem.

"Nick or no Nick, I'm not staying in here," Germ huffed, pushing past the group and making a grab for the front door handle. With all his little might he pulled and twisted, however the handle wouldn't move and the door refused to budge. "What the-?" he exclaimed, puzzled. Leaning back, he leveraged all his weight, but still, nothing. He beckoned to Billy. "Give me a hand here, will you?"

Billy aided Germ, but it was no use; the sole gateway to the outside refused to open. Phil leaned in and examined the doorknob.

"Jammed perhaps," he said. "But it doesn't appear to be locked."

"No, no, no," Germ shook his head and - with a small running start - threw his meager weight against the heavy door. It didn't budge. Still, he attempted a second time. And a third. Eventually Billy grabbed his friend by the shoulders and pulled him back.

"It's not going to work! Face it, we need to find another way," he pleaded, hoping that the others wouldn't hear the distress in his voice.

Germ composed himself, but couldn't hide his upset. "I'm going to miss curfew and my mom's not gonna let me leave the house until college. All thanks to 'Chicken Chuck' and his jerk of a brother."

Chuck turned bright red and looked at his feet. Billy saw and clenched his fist, incensed.

"You're the one being the jerk right now," he countered. "It's not Chuck's fault his brother's a butt-faced tool."

"You're right, it's not Chuck's fault," Germ retorted, venom in his voice. "We're here because of your space cadet girlfriend."

Those were fighting words. Chuck and Phil exchanged an uneasy look. Billy felt his face flush hot.

"She's NOT my girlfriend," he spit back.

Hook, line and sinker. Germ smirked, and smugly crossed his arms. He'd hit a sore spot and knew it. Before he could truly twist the knife, a sudden and abrupt flash flickered throughout, and the lights came on.

Panic erupted. Chuck flinched and cowered, whereas Phil shielded his eyes. Billy and Germ instinctively leapt to the other's side, a temporary truce in a moment of hysteria.

It was then that the house, now illuminated, revealed itself for the first time.

The boys were standing in the middle of a grand foyer. Grand in the sense of scale, not appearance or upkeep. For like the exterior, the inside of Bryerwood House was old, rundown, and like a time capsule of a bygone era. Most distinctively, it was downright eerie.

Furnished in drab, grim coloring - browns, greys, and earth tones - the only hint of color was the blood red curtains that accented the walls, breaking up the faded paper that hung peeled in patches. Darker spots, presumably mold, drew an unsightly pattern. The centerpiece of it all was a large, winding staircase, which was far from functional. The middle had collapsed, leaving a gaping and insurmountable gulf between the lower steps and the upper landing, hindering access to the shadowy, unknown stories above. Unmarked doors lined the other walls, as did heavy, antiquated wooden furniture and decor. Stale, and untouched by natural light; the only two windows in the room were fastidiously boarded up. And, coating the entire space, layers of cobwebs and dust, lit by foggy glass sconces and a smattering of waxen candles. The inside of the house was indeed as creepy as the exterior suggested it to be. Neglected and decayed, it was difficult to imagine that anyone had set foot inside this forsaken place for decades, if not a century.

The boys shared a collective shiver as they surveyed their surroundings. Lying in bed on dark nights, the wind howling outside and the full moon alight, they'd all imagined what the inside of the house might look or feel like, and how they would react if - heaven forbid - they ever found themselves within its walls. Kids told campfire stories describing the darkened halls, creaking doors, and ghostly wails. An endless well of nightmarish details. Regardless, even the most vivid accounts didn't do justice the actual *feeling* of being in Bryerwood and seeing the reality up-close. But what the boys saw next shook them to the core, making it feel as if all the air had been sucked out of the room.

Crumpled and lying on the faded and stained wool rug, was a foreboding omen, to say the least.

"S-s-speaking of Vanessa,' Phil stammered, pointing with one shaky hand. "Am I correct in thinking that might be hers?"

It was Vanessa's witch hat.

CHAPTER 16

Simple Trinkets

"**H**er... hat," the words escaped Billy, in a choked whisper.

You could hear a pin drop, it was so quiet. As if being stuck inside Bryerwood House wasn't enough, now the boys found themselves confronted by a terrifying possibility; Vanessa was in the house, and something bad had happened to her. And if the bad stuff could get to Vanessa, a girl known for embracing the gruesome and morbid, any one of them could be next.

Billy wished he could trade all the Halloween candy he'd ever collected to not be trapped inside of Bryerwood. Except wishing wouldn't help him and his friends right now; he needed to act. So, gathering his courage, he tightened his Danger Kevin cape around his shoulders.

"She's still here. Somewhere in this house. And we have to find her."

Germ shook his head adamantly. "Here it is, the final straw. You've officially lost it, my friend." He waved an arm, gesturing to the room. "What we *need* to find is a way out of The Addams Family's summer home."

Now it was Billy's turn to shake his head. "She's new in town. Has no idea what she's getting into. We can't just abandon her."

"We can and we should," Germ snorted. "I'm not breaking curfew because the school weirdo wants to compare boiled newt recipes with the Boogeyman."

Billy threw up his hands, exasperated. "Just admit it, Germ!" He exclaimed. "You're scared. Like the rest of us."

"*Scared?* Of what?!" Germ spit the words, affronted.

"I don't know! Of the things that every twelve-year-old kid is still scared of and doesn't want to admit to. You know. The things we're ALL afraid of."

Germ crossed his arms, defensive. "Speak for yourself."

"Fine. I will." Billy cleared his throat. "I'm tired of you always giving Chuck a hard time, calling him a baby or criticizing him for being afraid. Trying to score points while you put him down to make yourself feel good. You're no better than Noogie Nick."

"I'm fine, it's fine!" Chuck squeaked.

"No, it isn't," Billy shook his head. "Germ, you were just as scared as I was that day in the yard. And you're scared now, which is why you won't look for Vanessa. Admit it."

"Ha-ha-ha!" Germ feigned laughing. "Good one, Bill. First of all, I'm Chuck's friend, he *knows* I'm only joking. Second, why don't I show you just how 'scared' I actually am." He cupped his hands to his face and threw back his head, calling out. "Hell-oo!" Germ's voice echoed through the foyer.

"Shh!" Phil reprimanded, his eyes darting around the room. "What are you doing?!"

Germ strolled over to a bronze bust of a man's head. Flippantly, he threw an arm around the bust's shoulders like they were old friends, and pantomimed giving it a wet willy. "Take that you old fart!" He grinned mischievously. "Doesn't seem so scary to me, Bill!"

Billy glared back as he watched Germ stride across the room and stop at a heavy oak curio cabinet adorned with strange and old knick-knacks. Germ set his sights on a small wooden doll. Perhap once beloved by a child, the doll's decorative paint job had faded over time and almost completely worn off. Whether from wear and tear or most likely age, the doll's dress was frayed and yellowed, and the toy bore a number of scratches and marks.

"Really Bill," Germ said. "If I'm as scared as you say I am, would I lay one single finger on some freaky, probably straight-up possessed doll?" Maintaining eye contact, Germ grabbed the doll and held it up, like a freshly caught prize trout.

"Wow," he said, rolling his eyes. "I can't believe it. I'm so sca-"

There was a sudden flash of blinding light, and Billy, Chuck and Phil recoiled back, shielding their eyes. When the light acclimated, the small wooden doll was lying on the ground, discarded.

"What just happened?" Phil groaned, rubbing at his eyes.

"Germ!" Chuck cried out. "He... he's-"

"Gone," Billy whispered

Once again, the boys found themselves in a situation that went from bad to worse, without explanation. Only moments ago Germ was goading his friends, but, in the flick of switch, he had mysteriously disappeared.

CHAPTER 17

Shaken Up

"**G**erm!" Billy called out, his voice croaking. "Germ, where are you?"

Phil ran to every door in the room and inspected the handles. "All of these doorknobs have layers of dust; that means they're untouched." He did a re-lap and tried opening the doors. "And, as I suspected, all locked."

Chuck interjected. "Maybe there's a trap door? I saw a movie once where the kids escaped through a trapdoor, only to find-" he caught himself and shuddered. "Only to find that the killer was... waiting for them, beneath." As he uttered the words, the color drained from his face.

Billy gulped and carefully approached the spot where Germ had last stood. Gently, he nudged the doll away with his toe and gave three stomps in its place. There was no hollow sound, meaning no trapdoor.

"Nope. Solid ground beneath." Billy peered up at the unreachable second floor landing and hollered. "Germ, if this is a prank it's not funny!"

"It's the house," Chuck said shakily. "The house is doing this."

"Be reasonable, Chuck," Phil replied. "As creepy as Bryerwood is, a house can't make a person disappear."

Almost on cue, the overhead lanterns and sconces began to sputter, and the candle flames flickered. An invisible and angry tempest possessed the room, blowing gusto and threatening to extinguish the little light the boys had. As quickly as it came on, the flickering intensified. Like a pot of water reaching its boiling point, the entire house began to shake. Not enough to send anyone off-balance, but just enough that the trinkets and statues throughout the room rattled in place, and the paintings and decor on the walls jostled, swinging to-and-fro. Billy held his arms out to stabilize and Phil grabbed hold of the staircase railing. Poor Chuck was rendered helpless. Flailing, panicked.

"Bryerwood House got Germ like it got Vanessa!" Chuck cried out. Reflexively and without thinking twice, he grabbed an ornate lantern perched on a nearby sideboard, and hugged it close. "And the house wants-"

Another flash of light enveloped the room, this one brighter than the last. With it came an almost cleansing effect. The chaos quickly subdued. The shaking stopped. As swiftly as the calamity had come on, it ended, and the foyer returned to normal; or whatever could be deemed normal by the standards of Bryerwood.

Dazed, Billy rubbed at his eyes. When his vision re-focused, he took in his surroundings and let out a gasp.

There on the floor was the ornate lantern, the one Chuck had so desperately clasped as a last ditch lifeline. And Chuck-

Chuck was no longer in the room.

CHAPTER 18

To Read or Not to Read

"We need to act fast. Figure out what caused Germ and Chuck to disappear before we're next," said Phil, his voice wavering slightly despite the conviction of his words.

"Got it," Billy replied. He was shaken up and quite frankly scared out of his wits, but Phil was right. They needed to find a way out of Bryerwood, but couldn't do so without first finding Germ, Chuck and Vanessa, and also being cautious that they didn't follow suit.

"I have a theory," Phil began. "That Germ vanished because he picked up that doll, and likewise Chuck the lamp." His expression turned grave. "Billy, while you're looking, don't touch *anything*."

The realization washed over Billy. Of course! Phil, brilliant as ever, had drawn a connection and it made total sense. As outrageous as it sounded, the act of picking up items was triggering some strange phenomena. Far-fetched, but given what he'd seen already tonight, Billy was inclined to believe anything. "Don't touch anything," he repeated.

"There's a chance the answer to this puzzle is hidden some-where in this room," Phil said, scanning a cabinet that held a cache of dusty old books. Wearing his costume, he looked as if he could be from the same time the books were originally printed. "We can divide and conquer. Look for anything that feels out of the ordinary."

"So just about anything and everything in Bryerwood House. I'll try." Billy made his way over to the opposite wall. Lined with old paintings and pictures, it was a vast contrast to Billy's own home filled with photos of family trips to the Grand Canyon, and quaint paintings of bright, sunny cottages. Instead, the walls of Bryerwood were adorned with faded portraits of sullen, frowning people, and dated photographs taken at strange and grim locales. Billy shuddered at one picture in particular; it was especially eerie to see photos taken here, at Bryerwood. A sepia-toned, timeworn photograph showed a family of five posed on the Bryer-wood lawn. None were smiling. Centered in the back was a man in a dark tweed suit. To his left in an outdated style of dress was a plain looking woman, and to his right was a gangly teenage boy, the spitting image of the man. Standing in front were two identi-cal twin girls. *Did they live here once?* Billy thought. *Had they known the truth about Bryerwood?*

Billy's pondering was soon interrupted. At the other end of the room, Phil had made a breakthrough. "Billy!" he called. "Come get a load of this."

So he went to join Phil who had left the bookcase and was now examining something in the far corner. Judging by the glint in Phil's eye, Billy could tell his friend was especially excited by this discovery. Although he was generally reserved in his demeanor, there were two things that could rile Phil up; baseball and knowledge.

"Look," Phil beckoned Billy closer. There, in the corner of the room, was a small wooden lectern, large enough to hold only one thing; a very, very, very old book. Albeit weathered, worn, and the pages yellowed, the book was the kind with fancy gold edging. Etched on the cover were three words.

"'The Way Out,'" Billy read aloud. He paused, in thought. "Do you think it's referring to the house?"

"Perhaps," Phil replied. "Would certainly make sense in our predicament." As he spoke, his eyes never left the book. He was transfixed.

"So then... we should read it?" Billy asked.

"That's where it gets complicated. If we're operating under my theory that Chuck and Germ disappeared having picked up items in this room, then no, we shouldn't read it."

"Right, don't read, got it," Billy nodded.

"Unless," Phil went on, his eyes still glued to the book. "Whoever or whatever is controlling this elaborate scheme knows that we, the subjects, would have caught on by now. It's a little *too* on the nose. Which makes me question whether this is a test of agency, to see if we'll defy the rules we think to be true. In that case it's a double reversal. Which means that the answer to our problem - "The Way Out" - might *actually* lie within this book, and we'd be fools not to read it."

Billy was growing confused and losing track of Phil's logic.

"So you're saying we *should* read it?"

"No."

"Then don't?"

"... Also no."

Billy shook his head. Usually he chalked up any lack of understanding on his part to Phil being a brainiac, however in this case his friend just wasn't making any sense.

"Phil, I think you might be too smart for your own good sometimes." Billy stepped away, expecting Phil to follow suit... but he didn't. Instead, Phil stood, hovering over the book, mesmerized.

"Phil?"

"I have to know, Billy. Whether it's a trick or the real thing. I need to know." And with that, Phil reached for the book, a voracious look on his face as he lifted it from the lectern.

"No!"

Gingerly, Phil flipped the cover open, turning to the first page. His eyes wide with anticipation. Billy lunged forward, reaching, attempting to knock the book from his hands.

"Billy, it-"

But it was too late. Faster than the last two instances, there came a flash of blinding light. When the dust settled the book lay abandoned on the ground, and Phil had evaporated into thin air.

CHAPTER 19

The Mysterious Stranger

Billy wished that he was anywhere else instead of separated from his friends and trapped in Bryerwood, at the mercy of whatever dark force was chipping away at them one-by-one. On what was supposed to be the best night of their young lives, the first parent-free Halloween. Events had taken a nightmarish wrong turn, to say the least. Billy was alone and exposed, without a plan or next step to take.

Maybe, he thought, *I should just pick up that crystal globe over there, or that gross melted candle, or that weird frog statue.* More than likely he'd find himself in the same fate that befell his friends, but then he wouldn't be stuck in this creepy room without a hope.

As Billy contemplated his very bleak and very limited options, he caught a glimpse of something in the corner of his eye; Vanessa's witch hat, the one that had instigated the blow-out between Germ and him. Tired and unnerved, Billy walked over to the hat, bent down, and picked it up.

He winced, preparing for the worst. But there came no flash of disorienting light, no magic. And yet, something remarkable did occur.

Slowly, and with a pained *CREAK*, the door at the very top of the room, to the right of the crumbled staircase, swung open. Beyond it lay a long dark hall, at the end of which shone a faint sliver of light.

With nowhere else to turn, Billy went.

One hand on the wall and the other outstretched before him, he proceeded, bracing himself for what might wait at the other end. With each step the dim glow increased slightly, guiding the way. Eventually Billy could make out that it was coming from a door ajar at the other end of the hall, light seeping through the crack. Upon reaching this door, he took a deep breath. Then, with great trepidation, Billy peered through the gap.

From this limited angle he could make out a sitting room, decorated with dark, heavy oak furniture that looked like it was made at least seventy years earlier, if not more. A fire crackled at the far end of the room, casting light and shadow throughout. The dark aesthetic of the foyer carried through, as ghostly portraits and weathered photographs lined the walls. Even more disturbing than the pictures were the other hanging adornments; stuffed and taxidermied animals, likely game from a hunt. A deer head hung above the fireplace. A baby bobcat posed on an end table. A small murder of crows suspended near the ceiling. One of the crows was perched in such a way that Billy thought it looked as if any second it might dive down and peck out his eyes.

Central to the room was the impressively large fireplace, framed by a heavy brick mantle. Dwindling embers flickered in the hearth, and it was then that Billy realized how cold it was inside the house. Under other circumstances, warming by a fire would feel fairly comforting right now.

As eerie as the room itself was, it was the sight in front of the fireplace that caused a shiver to run through Billy's entire body. Positioned just askew of the stonework was a well-worn wing-back armchair; the kind with scrolling arms and leather accents. And in this chair sat a figure, cloaked in shadow.

Without stirring or turning to face him, the figure addressed Billy. "Welcome, boy." The voice was a man's, rasping, solemn, and just shy of a whisper. "Welcome, to Bryerwood House," he croaked.

"My house."

CHAPTER 20

Basement

"Billy? Phil? Where are you guys?" Chuck called out meekly. "Germ, are you playing a joke?"

The lack of response caused his fear to deepen. Sure, Germ might find it funny to hide and tease him in a situation like this, but Billy and Phil would never. Reluctantly, Chuck accepted that he was alone, and strangely, standing at the bottom of a staircase. The rickety, bare bones kind that descends from the main floor down into a basement. In which he was.

Like the chipmunk he resembled, Chuck scrambled up the creaking stairs on all fours. When he got to the top he felt around in the darkness for a doorknob. There was none. Leaning his weight into the door, he pressed and pushed, but it was no use. The door wouldn't budge.

CLATTER. Clunking and banging sounds resounded in the distance.

"Guys?" Chuck peered out, shaking, his worst fears manifested. "It's me - Chuck."

Tiptoeing, he crept back down the staircase. The basement

was dingy and poorly lit, but Chuck's eyes were slowly adjusting. Absent was the lantern from the foyer that he had clutched so closely in a moment of terror. Now he had nothing to hold onto but his own wits. Which in Chuck's opinion, wasn't much.

Chuck scanned the room. As dark as it was, he could tell that the space was packed full. Piles and piles of old, moldy boxes. Moth-ridden clothes. Broken tools. Heirlooms. Trinkets and waxen statues. Paintings and furniture stacked high. Twisting rows of one person's treasures and another's junk.

Creeping as quietly as a church mouse, Chuck inched his way forward. Little by little he waded through the walls of clutter, searching for a sign of his friends. Terrified as he was, he was also struck by an intense feeling of curiosity and urge to explore; a fairly foreign sensation to Chuck who normally didn't stray far from the familiar and comfortable. But in this moment it helped to take stock of his surroundings.

Most of the stuff was destined for a future dumpster, but every once in a while something caught his eye. Not based on interest, but because it was unusual. In one instance, a large assortment of old wooden children's toys (the antiquated kind that he and his friends would scoff at). Beyond the toys stood a trio mannequin busts, the type a tailor would use to shape garments. From these mannequins hung crinoline dresses, archaic in style, even older than the kind of dresses Chuck's grandmother wore. Time hadn't been kind to these frocks; they were mildewed and frayed, shy of unraveling at the pull of a single thread.

Past the dresses was the haunting image of a broken baby's crib. For a second, Chuck thought he saw it rock and a chill ran down his spine. He shuddered hard.

It was then that Chuck realized he was moving deeper into the basement with little sign as to where his friends might be. Having mustered enough bravery for one night, he decided to go back to the entrance, curl up into a ball, and wait there. He turned around with the intention of retracing his path, but what he saw made him gasp; an entirely new, unrecognizable stretch of basement lay before him. Gone were the toys, mannequins, and crib, and in their place sat stacks and stacks of yellowed newspaper.

Chuck picked up one of the papers and read the date; September 18th, 1948. Over 40 years ago. *Who on earth would keep such old newspapers?* he thought.

Panicked, Chuck dropped the newspaper and headed down a different path. This time he found himself face-to-face with a row of what looked like animal cages. Varying in size, some with bent or warped bars, and all with broken latches. With one furry hand, Chuck wiped sweat from his brow, his anxiety at a fever pitch.

Taking a few cautious steps forward, he stopped at an extremely large cage and peered inside the door. Dirty floor. Gooey, blood-like stains. Scratch marks. *What was locked inside this cage,* Chuck wondered, *and where is it now?*

He didn't have long to question it, when another *CLATTER* sounded again, this time much louder and closer.

"Hello?" Chuck cried out. "Who's there?!"

Another *CLATTER*. Even louder. Even closer.

"S-s-state who you are," Chuck stammered, holding up his chipmunk paws in tight fists that looked much less intimidating than he had hoped. He listened intently.

The clattering stopped, only to be replaced by another sound. A new sound.

A deep, low *growl*.

Out of the corner of Chuck's eye he caught a shadow dancing

across the high basement wall. It was hulking, jagged, and down-right ferocious.

He gave a small yelp, quaking in his furry booties. Whatever was casting that shadow, Chuck didn't want to find out. With no-where to hide, he backed into the large cage. Summoning what little strength he could, he wrenched the rusted door shut. The sound of groaning metal-on-metal reverberated throughout the cavernous basement, signaling, exposing. The shadow reacted, darting forward, searching and flailing blindly for the source.

Closing his eyes tightly, Chuck wished more than anything that he was at home in his own bed, sheets pulled tight to his chin, worrying about the monsters he knew.

CHAPTER 21

Ghost in the Attic

P hil was able to deduce fairly quickly that, thanks to the strange phenomena occurring in the foyer, he had wound up in the Bryerwood attic. Like a master sleuth, he drew upon the context clues in his surroundings.

First, Phil noticed a set of collapsible stairs to his left, the kind that extend from the ceiling above and are accessed via a small square trap door. He made an effort to open the latch, but it was stubbornly shut and required a key.

Second, across the room was a small, high window. Phil could faintly make out the treetops and roofs of the neighborhood that Bryerwood House towered over.

Third, it just *felt* like an attic.

Stuffy, narrow, and a treasure trove worth of memories. Every object, every leather bound trunk, every gilded mirror told a story. Relics, stored and forgotten until a later generation would rediscover and judge their worth. Coating it all was a half century's worth of dust, and strings upon strings of cobwebs.

Afraid as he was, Phil's natural sense of curiosity overcame him. *No use just standing here*, he thought. And so, rather than wrestling with a trap door that had no intention of opening, he cautiously explored.

Close to the attic entrance was a small work table covered with the inner gears and mechanical workings of a dissected brass clock. Phil ran his fingers over the set of tools carefully laid out on the table. They were old, very specific to horology and clock repair. Some looked like they were obsolete, no longer in use by today's standards.

Past the work table was a stack of trunks. Atop one was a set of dried-out paints. Propped on a small easel, a half-finished canvas had collected a thin layer of dust. Phil could make out the painting beneath and it sent chills down his spine. It was painted from the perspective outlooking the small attic window, of the surrounding treetop and roofs.

His thoughts were interrupted by a strange noise from the opposite end of the room. Almost like a low, pained sob.

"Hello?" Phil called out. "Is someone there?"

A pause. And then another quiet cry.

Against his judgement, Phil waded past the stores of cast-offs and artifacts, moving toward the sound. Getting closer, he realized what lay tucked at the far end of the long room.

A four poster bed, replete with fancy velvet canopy. Piled with worn quilts and bed lace, it emanated a musty smell.

The worst part, the part that caught Phil off guard, was that it wasn't just a bed. There was someone in it.

A woman. Or what once was.

She was ancient, to say the least. For a second Phil wasn't sure if she was even alive, until he saw her frail body moving up and down with heavy, laborious breaths, bearing the weight of the boney hands that rested in a fold on her chest. Her hair, likely once raven and lush, was dry and dusty, resembling burnt straw. Skeletal, her flesh was gray and saggy, hanging from her bones. Her cheeks were sunken, and Phil could easily imagine the shape of her skull. Dressed in what might once have been a wedding dress although it was yellowed by time, complete with matching veil. All enveloped in the stench of decay. This morbid bride was by all accounts a living corpse.

Waves of fear rippled through Phil. He stopped and took a few deep breaths. Mind racing, he willed himself to slow his thoughts and think clearly; as long as the woman stayed in bed, undisturbed, he could slowly make his way to the attic entrance and plot an escape from there.

Without breaking focus on the bed and its occupant, Phil started to slowly back away toward the opposite side of the attic. Little by little he was making progress, until-

CRASH! Phil backed into a rickety end table, sending a pile of bronze pots clattering to the ground.

He froze in place. There was a long pause in which the only audible sound was his own rapid heart beat, all but threatening to leap from his chest.

And then he heard it again - the low crying sound. Only this time Phil knew exactly where it was coming from.

The old woman was still in the bed, but now her mouth was agape. Her jaw hung like a window shutter that had barely survived a hurricane. Rolling out lifelessly, her tongue was black and covered in mold. The crying sound she made was guttural and screeching at the same time. Strangely the rest of her face was passive, save for one key change; her eyes were now open. Pale, and milky white in color.

Slowly, the bride began to rise in the bed to a seated position, stirring a layer of dust into the air around her. Phil tried to speak, but no words came out. He backed away, this time knocking an entire stack of books over. When he did, the woman's head slowly turned to face his direction.

"Fred... er... ick..?" The corpse spoke in a low, creaking tone. As she did, her mouth moved as if on a hinge, like a puppet's. *"Are... you there... my... love?"*

"Th-th-this is Ph-phil," he stammered.

"Freder... ick." She spun at the waist, swinging her lower half, preparing to dismount the bed. The air was completely filled with dust now. As she rustled the blankets around her, a swarm of dark bugs and maggots scattered across the bedspread, and onto the bride herself. But she paid them no mind; her attention was focused on Phil.

"You've... come... back to... me... " the woman groaned. Everything about her produced a *creaking* sound, from her voice to her body. Her milky white eyes were fixated, unblinking on Phil.

The bride took one labored step forward to stand, and Phil thought he heard something snap. Yet she continued forward, her legs rigid like wooden stilts.

"Mon chéri..."

Reaching out, the ghoulish woman moved toward him, yet Phil managed to evade as a rotting index finger fell off her hand, hitting the ground with a *plop*. Covering his mouth to stifle a scream, he dodged away.

"Excuse me, I-I-I'm lost and I'll be leaving now." The hem on Phil's robe unraveled, tripping him up.

"No." The bride tumbled at him, like a cursed scarecrow come to life. With each step she gained more and more forward mo-

mentum. Bugs shook from her. Between sentences she let out pained screeches and her mouth twisted in a gnarled contortion. But she had one focus, and that was Phil.

"*Frederick. You will stay... with me.*"

CHAPTER 22

A Couple of Dummies

To say Germ was scared was an understatement. More like terrified to his very core.

Sometimes outwardly tough guys can overcompensate to hide underlying insecurities, and Germ was no exception. Like Chuck, he was afraid of the dark. So much so that, since the incident with the baseball, he'd slept with his bedroom light on. Every night. But unlike Chuck, Germ did everything in his power to hide this from his friends, since at this age he'd be mocked for it and called a baby. So he shielded and deflected, going as far as to tease poor Chuck, knowing deep down that he had it just as bad, if not worse. It wasn't the behavior of a good friend, and on several occasions Germ felt ashamed after. And though he put on a boisterous, defensive act, he had felt especially so when Billy called him out on it tonight.

Now, in this dark and strange place, he was unable to control the fear that ravaged his mind. The fear he had so derisively mocked poor Chuck for. Gone was Germ's tough guy veneer as he sniffled and called out for his friends, lower lip quivering.

"G-g-guys? Hello? Help? Who's there? A-a-anyone?"

No response. Germ felt a lump in his throat. He was all alone. Only moments before he'd been clowning and posturing, putting on a show. Then, before he could say "boo," everything went blindingly white and he could feel himself teleported. It defied the laws of, well... everything. Starting with basic architectural design.

Germ was now in what would be considered an old fashioned parlor room. Arranged in the center was a small velvet sofa and two armchairs. Heavy red drapes lined the walls. The place looked like something Germ had seen in an old movie; the type of room where a group of fancy party goers would retire for the evening to smoke cigars, have a glass of brandy, and discuss baseball and taxes. Sure enough, there was a mahogany bar on the far side of the room with shelves holding glass bottles of aged liqueurs. A pyramid of expertly stacked glasses was just waiting to be toppled. Next to it was a wooden cigar box, like the kind Germ's dad gave him to keep his baseball cards in. At the other end of the room was an impressive grand piano, polished and shiny black.

Germ wasn't scared of the room itself. In fact it was pretty neat, and under normal circumstances he would have relished in his surroundings, taking the unchaperoned opportunity to pretend he was a mobster smoking a stogie and negotiating a shady business deal. Yet all Germ could focus on was the unsettling fact that aside from not knowing how he got into the parlor, it appeared to him that the room didn't have a *door*.

There was about a foot of exposed wall from the floor to the bottom of the red drapes that lined the room. Any wall space that didn't have curtains was covered in bookcases or shelving. Germ ran to the side of the room and pulled at the curtains. He ran over to the bar and peered over the counter, but there was nothing on the other side. Panicked, he staggered and spun in place, unsure where to go, or what to do. And that's when he heard a disembodied voice speak out.

"Looking for something?"

It was a man's voice, but higher pitched and whimsical.

Germ spun around, looking for the source. "Hello? Who's there?" he asked, timidly. As far as he could tell there was no one else in the room. And if someone *had* entered when his back was turned, where did they enter from? The voice spoke again.

"Waddaya mean 'who's there?' Open your eyes, ya knucklehead!"

More panic, as Germ's head swiveled on his shoulders searching for the voice. To no avail.

Where was it coming from? For a moment, adrenaline overcame him and he ran frantically around the room, peeking behind furniture, desperately trying to find who was speaking.

And that's when he saw it.

Propped up against the back of the piano bench was a wooden ventriloquist's dummy. In the lowlight Germ hadn't noticed it before, but now it was all he could fixate on. Those dead, glassy eyes bore into his.

"Hey, where'd you come from?" he asked. Upon closer inspection he realized it was dressed almost identical to him: pinstripe suit with matching hat and red tie. Like Germ's Halloween costume, it was straight out of a 1930's mob movie. He approached the doll with trepidation.

"You're one of those dummies that people make talk. Is someone here with you?"

The puppet stared back at Germ, blank, motionless. Germ

found its wide laughing smile to be very unsettling.

"If s-someone is here, you b-better show yourself." As he said it, Germ could hear his own voice breaking.

"*Or what?*" the disembodied voice spoke again. Germ gasped, so startled he nearly tripped over himself.

"*Sounds to me,*" the voice goaded, "*like you're the one who needs to show himself… show himself OUT!*"

A high-pitched, maniacal cackle followed. Germ fell back in terror and scrambled backwards on his hands and elbows. That's when he realized where the voice was coming from.

The dummy was now standing on the piano bench, its once smiling mouth twisted downward.

Then it spoke. But there was no puppet master providing the voice or moving the mouthpiece; it came directly from the doll itself.

"*Nice threads. A fellow wise guy, eh? Who sent you? Was it the Barroni Brothers?! Sing, canary!*"

Shaking, Germ clutched at the lapels of his flimsy, store-bought costume. "W-w-what?" he stammered. "I don't know the Barroni Brothers! I'm just a kid."

Teetering, as if on stilts, the dummy leapt from the piano bench to a nearby chaise, then crossed it to an end table. Now at a height advantage, he towered over a helpless Germ who had shrunk down against an antique sofa.

"Stay back!" Germ cried out.

Instinctively, he reached into his pocket for whatever he could find, producing only a fake plastic gun, the one he'd used to roughhouse with Billy's dad. Hands trembling, he pointed the gun at the puppet. It didn't contain any actual bullets, not even BB's, but maybe it could pass enough to deter his advancer.

"I said, stay back. Or... or... I'll shoot."

"*I give, I give!*" The dummy raised its little wooden-jointed hands in the air, yielding. "*Quite the pea shooter you got there,*" the doll smirked, "*I'd expect no less from a Barroni. Good thing I came prepared.*"

Reaching behind its back, the puppet retrieved a very real, very lethal looking tommy gun.

"*Lemme check to see if it's loaded.*" Aiming the gun at the bar, the dummy FIRED, and a real bullet let loose, shattering the pyramid of glasses stacked on the counter. Germ cried out.

"*Would ya look at that,*" the evil puppet sneered as Germ trembled helplessly. "*Packs a bit of a punch. We's got ourselves a good old fashioned shoot-out!*"

The dummy laughed maniacally as Germ scrambled to his feet. Leaping from the table, the doll gave chase, brandishing the gun at Germ. And Germ - who felt a tsunami-sized wave of regret for every time he had ever belittled or snickered at Chuck's sensitive side - ran screaming, desperately searching for a door that didn't exist.

CHAPTER 23

Mr. Hyde

The dark figure in the armchair turned to face Billy.

"What brings you here, young man?"

Frightened and unsure how to respond, Billy decided to be honest. "My name's Billy. I-I'm looking for my friends," he said, doing his best to steady his voice.

"Is that so?" the man replied. It was phrased as a question, but there was no inflection in his voice. He turned in his chair as the fire flickered higher. Billy caught his first real glimpse of the stranger.

He looked to be around the age of Billy's dad, but much more weathered. His face was sunken, his jaw sharp, and his skin deeply lined with worry. Billy was alarmed at how tired the man looked. Hollow eyes with dark circles underneath, his skin a sickly pale green. In addition to his troubling visage, the man gave off an overly-anxious air.

"Not many people come looking for friends in this house."

The man stood and Billy could see that he wore trousers and a shabby suit jacket. In some spots there were stitches and patches, crudely mended, as if the man had made the repairs himself. He took a step toward BIlly, but then, almost as if catching himself, slumped back into his chair.

"My f-friend came trick-or-treating here," Billy stuttered. "But she disappeared, so we - my other friends and I - came after her." He paused for a moment, before continuing. "Have you seen her?"

The man was looking away, biting his lip and wringing his hands. Billy noticed that he was fixated on a grandfather clock that hung on the far wall.

"William, you seem like a commendable young person, a very upstanding boy. You and your friends have chosen an interesting night to visit this house. In fact, the most interesting night of the year. Unfortunately, it is also the *wrong* night."

Giving a weak smile, the man pointed to a serving cart near Billy. "Please son, will you bring me that vial there?"

Billy looked down at the cart and saw a selection of glassware and bottles containing an array of mysterious liquids. Among them was an ornate vial, shaped like a heart. "Y-yes."

The man nodded and then turned away, coughing as he did. Reaching for the vial, Billy cursed as his shaky hand knocked it over, spilling the contents. Thankfully the man's loud rasps and wheezes concealed the sound. Panicked, Billy swiftly refilled the vial from a decanter that held a similar liquid. He brought the vial to the man and handed it over.

"Thank you." Tipping his head back, the man downed the vial's contents. "Time is of the essence," he whispered, practically choking on his words. "This house-"

His speech was interrupted by another fitful cough. This scared Billy even more, and he drew his Danger Kevin cape around his shoulders. The man also looked afraid; his gaze darted more frequently now between Billy, the vial, and the clock. Billy noticed the time was one minute to midnight... much later than he thought.

"This house doesn't-"

Before the man could speak further, he began to cough again, hacking and gasping for breath. Violently. As he convulsed, he lurched forward from the chair once again.

"P-please, just tell me where I can find my friends," Billy pleaded, his courage wavering as he backed toward the door. The man continued to cough and heave, looking sicker and sicker now. His brow was covered in sweat and his limbs jerked in unnatural movements. Again, he stumbled toward Billy, knocking the empty vial to the ground and stepping on it, shattering the glass.

"*Vanessa...*"

And that's when the minute hand of the grandfather clock ticked over to twelve, and the loud chimes of the clock heralded the midnight hour. On cue, the man's entire body convulsed violently. He retched and his face contorted. Seizing and foaming at the mouth, he tore at his skin and clothes, clawing his own flesh. Eventually the man threw himself to the ground, spasming.

Billy watched, in a stunned silence. He should have run, but instead froze on the spot. There was nothing he could do but look on in horror as the man twisted and writhed in pain.

After some time the seizing stopped and the man collapsed to the ground in a crumpled heap, illuminated by the fading fire. Condition unknown, but Billy could tell he was still breathing.

"S-sir?" Billy asked, inching cautiously toward the stranger. "Are you okay?'

Silence. No response. Then, without any warning, the man's

left hand shot into the air. One by one, like a broken marionette, the rest of his limbs jutted out. He forced himself up in a clumsy stagger and twisted to a standing position, his body hunched. He turned to face Billy, and the young boy recoiled.

Staring, full of malice, was a person so vile that he barely resembled the man. His body was caked with blood; remnants of the scratches and wounds he'd inflicted upon himself. His skin was still the same sickly shade of green, but now, prominent purple veins ran down his face, neck and arms. The person standing before Billy was something wholly wretched and monstrous. Almost inhuman.

And somehow - Billy didn't know how - the man looked... *stronger.*

His gaze fixed on the boy. There was a sinister glint in his eye, and his mouth twisted into a sneer.

"He wasn't very fun, was he?" the man snarled. He spit every word as if it were dripping with poison. *"Weakling, without a nerve to his name."*

"Who?" Billy masked how frightened he was by leaning into his confusion.

"Him. The doctor." the man growled. *"But don't worry; he's gone now."* He rose to his full height, looming over Billy and looking absolutely deranged. *"I know what people say. About Bryerwood. What you and your friends must say..."*

"... Oh?" Billy backed away, fearful that even the slightest misstep in response could be triggering.

"And yet, you don't know, Billy. No one knows. How- how special it is. Those who avoid this house, those who willfully shun us... they will never know how special it is to be a part of it." Smiling devilishly, the man closed in on Billy, leaving him with nowhere left to turn, no

path of escape.

"Tell me something, Billy. Do you like to play baseball?"

CHAPTER 24

Bad Luck Chuck

C huck clutched at the rusted cage bars, the sole protective barrier between him and the monstrous creature that lurked nearby. When another unnerving growl sounded and the shadow reappeared, he scrambled to the middle of the cage and huddled there, doing his best to be as small as possible and inaccessible to any hands, talons, claws or tentacles that might try to reach through the bars.

Why, oh why, Chuck thought to himself, *did it have to be so dark?* It was bad enough when scary things happened in broad daylight, let alone in a frightening, unlit basement. Chuck's grandma once told him that many people are afraid of what they can't see or understand, but, once they experience the unknown up close, they look back and laugh at their unwarranted fear. Chuck had nodded along as she spoke, but secretly he felt that Gram was way off the mark.

Be brave, he told himself. He thought about what Germ would say if he saw Chuck now, and felt a defiant burst rise in his chest. If Germ was here, he would tell him to-

Growl. Closer. Right beside the cage. This one caught Chuck off-guard, and he let out an involuntary whimper. The whimper was met by a snarl, one that sounded almost pleased and mildly curious. Closing his eyes tightly, Chuck inhaled deeply, and drew from his shallow well of courage. He balled his chipmunk-gloved hands into tight fists.

CLANG. CLANG. Like an earthquake, an invisible force shook and rattled the entire. Chuck shrieked and toppled backwards.

That's when he saw *it*.

Emerged from the shadows and now crouched outside the cage, was a creature. Not an animal. A *creature*. Despite his bedtime fears, Chuck knew monsters weren't real, yet the thing that stood before him implied otherwise.

Even crouched on all fours, the beast was at least six feet tall. Hunched and rounded through the torso, its body was long, angular and malleable. Four bowed limbs jutted from it, bent and arched outward, spindly like a spider's legs. Its skin was ashen grey and covered in a mix of dark fur, scales, and spikes, as if the thing couldn't decide how to cloak itself, so settled for every available feature.

But the scariest part was the head. It resembled a longhorn skull, narrow and v-shaped. The eyes were hollowed, void of pupils, and in their place a black, black emptiness.

Snarling and breathing heavily, the creature leaned forward pressing itself against the bars and shaking the cage. Instinctively Chuck retracted, curling his body into a tiny ball. The monster jerked its head forward so its right eye peered through the cage bars. Chuck gave a yelp.

"*Tasty,*" snarled the thing "*To sup upon seasoned 'munk meat, provide me feast!*"

Chuck gasped. It could talk?! Sure, the way it spoke was very strange, but it was talking nonetheless.

"'M-munk meat?!' I-I'm not a chipmunk!" squeaked Chuck.

The beast eyed its prey and gave a skeptical growl. "*Munk to my eyes.*"

Chuck looked down at his furry body and matching paws. "I'm a boy, not a chipmunk! This is just a costume," he protested. In response the creature lunged at the cage, snarling. Chuck recoiled.

"*CHIP-MUNK,*" it growled.

Desperate, Chuck tugged at the costume to remove it... but it wouldn't come off. Chuck's grandmother had done *such* a good job making the suit that it was almost like a second skin. Had it not been for her assistance, he wouldn't have been able to climb into and fasten it in the back. Even the ears, seemingly held on by a crude string tie, were secured in place by some type of exotic knot that cemented them to Chuck's head, despite how hard he yanked at it. Under any other non-terrifying circumstance Chuck would have been impressed by his Gram's craftsmanship. Now he could only curse her talents as he was moments away from being devoured.

"No, no, no," Chuck whimpered quietly. "This isn't real! I'm not a chipmunk."

"*Less to talk, more to eat.*" The creature smiled, teeth bared in a savage grin.

Giving another squeak, Chunk ran to the back of the cage, as far away from the monster as he could get.

CHAPTER 25

A Deadly Reflection

Like Chuck, Phil was also in a very dire situation, pursued by the ghostly corpse of a woman who mistook him for her long-lost "Frederick." Creaking with movement, she enclosed in on him now, her putrid stench inescapable. Bugs fell from her hair and dress as she took each twitchy step.

"*Frederick... Frederick. C'est moi... my love...*" She lurched at Phil, offering her arms out as if about to clasp him in a deadly embrace.

"I'm n-n-NOT Frederick!" Desperate, Phil picked up a nearby wicker basket and threw it at the woman. It connected and she tumbled back a few steps. As she teetered and regained her footing, Phil surveyed his best options. To his right was a mirror; to his left, a rusty metal curtain rod.

The bride made a move at Phil. Reacting quickly, he grabbed the curtain rod and speared it forward, impaling her through the stomach.

She froze and looked down at the rod that protruded from her stomach. A swarm of bugs scrambled from the wound. In the place of blood, a dark goo oozed out. Phil looked on wide-eyed as the woman began to claw at it, trying to remove it. When it appeared nothing could be done, she dropped her attention from the rod as if feeling no pain and resumed her pursuit. The pole was driven deeper and deeper with every labored step, but her focus was on Phil, and only Phil. Terrified, he let go of the rod, and she momentarily swayed to-and-fro.

Phil felt a level of panic unbeknownst to him. He grabbed at any item within his reach and threw it at the bride, shattering antique vases, cracking porcelain dolls, and destroying delicate knick knacks and trinkets. But it was no use. Though the pole had slowed her down slightly, the undead woman wasn't stopping.

This was it. Cornered, Phil imagined the woman descending upon him, squeezing and sucking the life right out of him, locking him in her sickly clutches for all eternity. As they entwined she would weave her death through him and the maggots and bugs would infest his body, the rot spreading from her into him. The thought caused him to cry out, and, in one final act of self-preservation, Phil reached for the gilded mirror to his right. Cowering in place, he hoisted the shield over his back like a turtle shell, bracing for the bride's final embrace.

Except the smothering didn't come. Instead, the woman recoiled backwards, howling in agony. Screams so piercing that, had Phil not been holding the mirror, he would have covered his ears.

"*Mon dieu! ...Frederick!*" she shrieked.

Peering over the beveled edge he saw her thrashing wildly; bugs, bile, and putrescent flesh flying in all directions. In the shock of the moment, Phil couldn't pinpoint the source of her distress until he noticed she was trying to cover her face. Confused, he looked down at the mirror and realized what was disturbing her.

In the mirror was the reflection of a beautiful young woman wearing a sparkling, white lace dress, not too unlike the dress the decaying woman wore. Except the woman in the photo was vibrant and beautiful, her whole life ahead of her. On her face she wore a sad, secretive smile.

Steadying himself, Phil got to his feet and raised the mirror toward the ghoulish bride, like a lion tamer. She screeched and cried, sounds worse than nails on a chalkboard. The image of the young woman in the mirror grew clearer, stronger. As Phil pushed the bride back, she started to shrink. Melting. It began at her feet, then her knees buckled, next her torso. Soon her cries fell softer and muffled as her face began to melt away like hot wax. Although Phil found this all unsettling, he was no longer fearful for his life.

The last gasps of death gave way until all that was left was a mound of moldy old lace. So gross that even the last few bugs couldn't wait to scuttle away. Then, the reflection of the young woman in the mirror faded away.

Relieved and exhausted from the horror he had just experienced. Phil fell to the ground and sat panting, catching his breath. As he gasped for air he noticed something shiny sticking out of the pile of lace. Gingerly, he reached over and picked up the object.

It was a locket. Heart-shaped, like the kind given as a gift to a loved one. As old and rotten as the bride was, the locket was fairly well kept and gave off a shine.

Phil opened it and found two things inside. One was an old and well-worn, black-and-white photo of a man and a woman. Dark haired and handsome, the man wore a military-issued coat.

Linking his arm was the fair young woman he had seen in the mirror's reflection. Except this time her smile was not sad, but warm and hopeful. The man was also smiling, a smile of pride and happiness.

Phil ran his fingers over the photo and noticed an unusual bump beneath. Curious, he removed the picture and found that hidden behind it was a gold key. It gave Phil an idea.

He took the key to the attic door, put it in the notch, and unlocked it. The door *creaked* as he pulled it open. Lowering the stairs, Phil took a deep breath, then descended to the floor below.

CHAPTER 26

A Secret Way

"**I** got one more marble in this peashooter with your name on it!" the dummy cackled.

Grabbing a stained glass lamp, Germ threw it at his wooden adversary. "For the last time, I'm not a mobster! This is a Halloween costume!" he exclaimed.

The puppet dodged the lamp, but not without getting a few shards of glass lodged in its face from the projectile. Even so, it gave no reaction, save for its wicked smile turning to a malevolent grimace, as its painted brows furrowed.

Germ was running out of energy and ways to elude the doll. Now, he found himself between a sofa and a row of bookcases. He pulled a dusty book off a shelf and hurled it directly at his combatant.

"*Trying to throw the book at me, eh? What are you, a judge?!*" the dummy quipped, effortlessly dodging it.

In a last-ditch effort, Germ reached for what appeared to be one of the largest, heaviest books on the shelf; a brown leather tome bound with gold trim. On its spine read the title: "Literary

Excerpts and Other Passages." Old, but still in good condition. Except when Germ pulled at the book, it didn't budge.

"Huh?" he said, tugging at it. Perplexed, he kept pulling, but the book was stuck. He was so distracted that he didn't notice that dummy pointing the gun straight at him. Germ gasped.

"Say your prayers, pipsqueak!" The doll squared up the shot, and pulled the trigger. Germ winced, bracing for the inevitable.

But there came no pain, no numbness or shock. He patted himself down for a wound but found none. Out of the corner of his eye he caught his reflection in the bar mirror; perfectly centered in the front of his fedora was a smoking bullet hole. Seeing it made Germ feel lightheaded.

Tossing the empty gun aside, the dummy gave a stiff shrug. *"Typical me, I always set my sights too high! But don't worry your pretty head; I've got a back-up plan."*

Reaching into the lapel of its little jacket, the puppet produced something equally terrifying; a big, sharp knife. Laughing maniacally, it brandished the knife, swiping at the air, and closing in on Germ.

"You tell those Barroni Brothers that they can keep their money! In exchange I get a pound of your flesh. Then we'll call it Even-Steven." Germ was still clueless as to who these mobsters were. Even so, there was zero chance he'd get to explain the misunderstanding to a murderous doll come-to-life.

This is it, Germ thought. *I'm toast. Kaput. Done-zo. And the worst part? My sister's going to get all my stuff.*

And that's all it took. The idea of Becca getting free reign of his cassettes, VHS tapes, posters and collectibles gave Germ a new-found sense of determination. This might be the end, but he would go out swinging, driven by pure and utter sibling rivalry.

Becca might get his stuff, sure, but he wasn't about to lay down and die to let that happen.

With both hands he grabbed the stuck brown leather book. Using his full strength and leveraging his weight, Germ gave one final pull. It was enough, and, while the book didn't leave the shelf, it was enough force to yank it downward, at a forty-five degree angle.

Almost magically, the entire shelf began to rotate, like a revolving door, spinning on its axis and taking Germ - who was still clutching the book - with it. As the shelf spun, the side of the bookcase connected with the dummy, knocking its light wooden body clear.

After a few wild rotations, the bookcase lulled to its original place flush against the wall. The brown leather book was intact, but Germ was nowhere to be seen.

The puppet stared for a moment, dumbfounded. Then, casually tossing the knife over one shoulder, gave a dispassionate shrug. *"Ah well,"* the dummy said aloud. *"Probably wasn't the right guy anyway."*

CHAPTER 27

Unexpected Diversion

"A baseball... Trespassed..."

The man spasmed and convulsed as he spoke. His eyes, bloodshot and wild, gave off an otherworldly look of demonic possession.

"It was an accident," Billy said, trembling as he spoke. Terrified, he found himself rambling. "We had nowhere else to play, Noogie Nick was at the park. I didn't think Germ could even hit it over the fence, and, and-"

"And nothing. This house... this house..."

Stopping short in his tracks, the man seized where he stood. The whites of his eyes rolled back in his head and he screeched out horrific, inhuman sounds unlike anything Billy had ever heard. His body bent backward in a painful twist, almost as if he was trying to restrain himself.

"This house," the man spat out, composing himself. *"I am its keeper. And it keeps me."*

The way he spoke sent a chill through Billy. Using language that implied Bryerwood House was a living thing.

"Y-y-you can just let me go," Billy pleaded. "I won't tell any-one."

"You're right. You won't."

Bellowing with rage, the demon lunged at Billy. Crazed, snarl-ing and clawing at the boy, unrelenting, like a rabid dog, red-eyed and foaming at the mouth. Billy fell backwards and, with an artful dodge, was able to scramble away.

CRACK! Before the man could strike, a nearby bookcase de-tached from the wall, and spun out wildly. Hit by blunt force and momentum, the man went tumbling backwards, knocked uncon-scious. And there, gripping the side of the bookcase, hanging on for dear life, was a young boy dressed in a pinstripe suit.

"Germ?" asked Billy, stunned, rising back to his feet.

"Billy?" replied Germ, looking from the crumpled body of the man on the ground, to his friend.

There was a brief pause, after which both erupted in joy and hugged.

"Germ!"

"Billy!"

"Are Chuck and Phil with you?"

"Nope. Can't even imagine what crazy stuff they might be up to."

Billy nodded. "We need to find them. Now."

"Right." Germ gave the man on the ground a soft tap with his toe. "What's the deal with this guy? He alive?"

Billy could tell that the man, although knocked out cold, was indeed still breathing. "Yes. Which is why we have to get out of here."

Germ nodded emphatically. "Tell me about it. I just spent fif-teen minutes playing tag with a violent puppet who mistook me for an Italian mobster."

Billy paused. "I have several questions but now isn't the time. Follow me."

Stepping warily over the man, the two made haste for the door to the hall, and Billy swung it open without hesitation.

Waiting on the other side was a mysterious figure, in a dark hooded cloak. Having let their guard down, Billy and Germ gasped and froze in place at the sight. Silently, the figure extended one hand, and, with the other, pushed back his hood.

"Heya fellas," Phil said, smiling broadly. "Long time no see."

CHAPTER 28

Reunited... Sort Of

After the initial wash of relief and some quick hugs, the boys huddled to the side of the hall and quickly compared notes. Billy told them about the cursed man and the mysterious vial. Describing in detail her horrid visage and nightmarish howl, Phil shared his own frightening scenario in which the undead bride had tried to possess him for her own. Of course neither of their retellings could match Germ pantomiming the dummy's murderous rampage, taking some liberties to exaggerate his own level of bravery.

"I can confidently say, my suspicions are confirmed; this house is haunted," Germ said.

Billy laughed and shook his head. Germ gave a small smile, but then quickly looked down at his hands, feeling ashamed. "You guys were right. I have been acting like a dumb booger-faced jerk, haven't I?"

Phil shrugged. "Not my exact word choice, but yeah; close enough."

"I'm sorry." Germ wore an earnest expression, a rarity for him.

"Sometimes I feel like I have to prove myself and... I go too far. Bill, I'm scared too."

"It's okay." Billy knew it took a lot for Germ to say this. He placed a hand on his friend's shoulder. "Thick and thin, we've made it through. Remember that time those kids from Meadowvale trashed your forest fort?"

Germ cracked a smile at the memory. "Yeah. And you guys helped me work a week straight to rebuild it. So when they attacked again-"

"-We could hide stink bombs in it," they said in unison, laughing.

Billy gestured at himself and Phil. "We'll always have your back, Germ. But you need to have ours."

Germ nodded. "I promise I will. Always. For now, we gotta find Chuckers."

"Perhaps I can be of help there." A voice spoke. The boys turned in surprise and almost leapt out of their skin when they saw a familiar face.

Silhouetted at the end of the darkened corridor, hand on a hip and looking only slightly worse for wear, was Vanessa.

"What'd I miss?" she asked.

Billy was at a loss for words and he could tell by the expressions on his friends' faces that they were also stunned by this new development. "Vanessa! Where have you been?" he blurted.

"Are you okay?" Phil asked.

"You're alive!" Germ exclaimed. Despite his pledge to change, he was still a little short in the tact department.

Vanessa crossed the hall toward the boys. She still wore her witch costume, but gone were the prosthetics and of course, her hat.

"Surprisingly, so are you. It's been a trying night, to say the least," she said, her voice grave.

"I'll bet," Germ replied.

"I hate to say it, Vanessa..." Billy began, "but we warned you. Bryerwood's bad news."

Vanessa nodded, earnestly. "And you were right. The things I've seen... where to begin..." she looked beyond the boys, lost in thought, as if replaying her harrowing ordeal in her mind. Billy, Phil and Germ waited with baited breath for her to recount.

"It all started, of course, with the trick-or-treating," she began. "Up the stairs I went. Alone on the porch, of course. No other kids in sight. No doorbell to speak of. So I knocked."

"And?" Phil pressed, his eyes wide.

"And... nothing," she shrugged. "At least not at first. I was prepared to turn around and leave when suddenly, the door just-"

"-Opened?" finished Billy.

"Exactly. And I couldn't resist the allure, so I went right in. But there was no one behind the door, or even in the entryway. Not a single soul."

"Did you look around?" Billy asked. "At all the creepy pictures and decorations?"

Vanessa nodded. "Mm hmm. Such an interesting collection. Naturally I was intrigued."

"Tell me you didn't touch anything..." Germ frowned, remembering.

"How did you know?" she replied. "I saw a statue of a magpie. With jeweled eyes, and gold talons. My curiosity was piqued. Meeting a magpie on the road is a sign of bad luck. But what about an avenue? Or a cul-de-sac? Do the same rules apply? Anyway, I picked up the statue to examine it, but before I could there was a flash of light. Blinding. Moments later I was somewhere else entirely."

"Where… where were you?" Phil asked.

"The basement. And that's where I saw Chuck."

Billy gasped. Phil and Germ were also shocked by this revelation. A brief, dramatic pause, followed by excited chatter and frantic questions.

"Did you talk to him? Is he okay?! Where is he now?"

Vanessa waved her hands, motioning for the boys to let her talk. They fell silent.

"Chuck is still down there. Held captive in the basement by a ferocious creature," Vanessa hesitated. "… A monster."

The boys eyed one another. Phil was biting his lip and the color had drained from Germ's face.

Billy gulped. If the rest of the house was any indication, the basement promised to be ten times as scary. But there was no other option.

"We have to go get him. We have to get Chuck."

"It won't be easy, and not without risk. The basement is a perilous place, but I can show you the way to him," Vanessa said.

"Let's do it." Billy held his hand out flat. Phil nodded solemnly and placed his hand on top. Germ gave a dramatic pause, then, letting out a playful sigh, threw his arms up in a mock begrudging gesture. "Next year I'm gonna stay home and give out apples with Chuck's grandma. Don't even ASK me to trick-or-treat, cause I won't do it," he said, smirking as he added his hand to the pile.

"Okay, Germ," Billy said, returning the grin. "We won't."

Now Billy turned and looked expectantly at Vanessa who was still standing off to the side. Arms crossed and visibly uncomfortable, she shifted her weight from foot-to-foot.

With his free hand, Billy gave a small salute. "All for one and one for all?"

"... Me?" she asked, nonplussed.

"Takes a team to battle ghouls and monsters," Phil replied.

Vanessa gave a pensive pause, unsure how to respond. Then, with a nod, she added her hand in solidarity.

Steeling themselves, the four tread uneasily down the dark hallway, united in the face of fear to save their friend.

CHAPTER 29

Vanessa

T he hall let out into the front foyer which was still as creepy as the boys remembered it. Vanessa led the charge and stopped in front of a newly - particularly decrepit-looking - unlocked door.

"This way," she urged, as she crossed the threshold and beckoned them down a flight of creaky stairs. The boys stayed close behind, on tiptoe no less, so as not to make too much noise.

Stopping about halfway down and nearly causing a collision, Vanessa abruptly turned to face Billy, Germ and Phil. "It's dark down here and like walking through a maze," she informed them. "Try to keep up."

"'Keep up?'" Germ repeated. "Is it a race?"

"You'll see." Vanessa continued down the stairs and the boys followed.

And she was right. As far as the eye could see, the cavernous basement was filled with stuff. Junk and treasure alike. Like the rest of Bryerwood it was also dark and therefore difficult to see. Save for the random flickering of a lamp or lantern somewhere in the distance, there wasn't too much light. As they walked among the piles and weaving paths of old furniture, books, toys, tools, boxes and debris, Billy caught himself anxiously imagining all the possible horrors hidden beyond each corner, and the dancing shadows on the walls and surfaces didn't help.

"Who do you think all this junk belongs to?" Germ whispered.

"Past owners, probably?" Phil offered.

Billy grimaced. "Some poor saps who bought the place, got more than they bargained for, and ditched it before they could get their stuff."

Vanessa stopped unexpectedly again and gave a hand signal to halt. The boys froze in place. She pressed a hand to her lips and tilted her head, listening intently.

"If I tell you to hide, you hide. Got it?"

Germ looked from Vanessa to his friends, wide-eyed. "From what?"

Before she could respond, a low yet booming GROWL echoed throughout the basement. Not the growl of a dog or even a bear. Something much, much worse.

"Hide!" Vanessa hissed. In a panicked scramble, Phil dipped inside a rusted oil drum turned on its side, Germ sought cover beneath a nearby tarp, Billy crouched under a fallen bookcase, and Vanessa camouflaged herself behind a jumble of old coat racks. Helpless, they waited. Until once again, came another rumble, quieter and less bombastic. With it, a large shadow flashed across the room, crawling like a prowler in the night; pacing back and forth, searching. Eventually it subsided and the shadow disappeared, and with it the growling. Billy and his friends, albeit frightened, let out sighs of relief.

"What the heck was that?" Germ whispered.

"You don't want to know," Vanessa replied, moving swiftly through the clutter.

"I do," Billy retorted. "We need to know what we're up against here."

"No time right now for explanations. Need to move."

Vanessa took off and the boys had no choice but to follow. She was moving quicker now, darting back and forth between boxes of bric-a-brac, sheets strung up to dry and then forgotten, and furniture, stacked to the ceiling in places. Billy was almost running to keep up, and Germ - terminally short-limbed - was having the toughest time of all three, struggling in the back.

Vanessa stopped against a decorative partition. She turned to the boys and opened her mouth to say something. Before she could, she was interrupted by another harrowing growl.

"Hide!" she whispered once more.

The options were sparse this time. Billy was forced to backtrack some and take cover inside a broken armoire. He waited, peering through the door hinges as the shadow moved overhead. Like before, it lingered, on the hunt. Except this time whatever it was came close enough that Billy could hear the sound of heavy clawed footsteps scratching the floor, and the wild animalistic breathing that filled the space between growls.

When the shadow passed and the coast seemed clear, Billy stepped out from the armoire. Phil and Germ followed suit, exiting their hiding spot under a mannequin's tent-like crinoline skirt.

"That was close," Phil said.

"Yep. Too close," Billy agreed, dusting his stuntman costume off. "What is that thing, Vanessa? Those aren't the sounds your average family dog makes."

No response. He gave it a beat. "Vanessa?"

Silence.

Vanessa was gone.

CHAPTER 30

Chipmunk Chuck

"Did anyone see where she went?"

Phil and Germ shook their heads. Billy had been so distracted looking for his own cover that he hadn't even seen which direction Vanessa went.

"Could that... that *thing* have gotten her?" he asked, gulping.

"Wouldn't we have heard?" Phil pointed out. "A scream? Her calling out to us?"

Billy considered this. "Unless it snuck up on her. Stealthy. Before she could react."

"I don't intend to wait and find out," Germ replied, grimly.

"We're sitting ducks here," Phil agreed. "We won't find Vanessa or Chuck unless we keep moving."

As terrible as he felt picking up and moving on, Billy knew his friends were right.

"All right. Looks like we have no choice."

With Vanessa gone, Phil and Germ looked to Billy expectantly as the de facto search party leader. But taking up her mantle wasn't easy; Billy wasn't sure which way to go, and the basement and its winding labyrinth of relics gave no clue or indication. Still, he chose a path and stuck to it, and they ventured onward.

Several minutes passed without appearance from the shadow creature, but also without any sign of Chuck or Vanessa. Tensions peaked when, rounding a corner, the trio passed a broken baby's crib that looked awfully familiar. Phil stopped, a sinking expression spreading across his face.

"I hate to say it, but... we might be going in circles."

Indeed they were. And had been for some time.

Germ nodded. "It's so dark. And everything looks the same," he paused for effect. "The same as in 'creepy.'"

Billy was frustrated. Catching a glimpse of himself in a dulled mirror didn't help. His resplendent white and red Danger Kevin costume was muddied and grimed from the night's harrowing events, and his helmet scuffed. He was the opposite of a champion stuntman, unable to conquer all, and in that moment didn't feel like much of a leader.

But it was then that a spark of hope presented itself. For in the same mirror, just over his shoulder, Billy saw something. Or rather, someone.

"Chuck?" he spun around, alarmed.

There, across the way, was the silhouette of a small and furry-looking figure. The mysterious individual gave a wave, then turned tail and ran in the opposite direction. Without hesitation, Billy started to chase after.

"C'mon guys!" he exclaimed, motioning to a confused Germ and Phil. "It's Chuck!"

"What?!" hissed Germ, jogging to keep up.

"Chuck!" Billy called again, his voice rising precariously above the whisper he'd been trying to maintain. "Buddy, slow down, it's us!"

The figure was moving fast, much faster than Billy could recall ever seeing Chuck move; dodging and weaving among the bestrewn basement clutter with athletic dexterity. *Never seen Chuck do this when our team needs him to round second*, Billy thought.

After a seemingly endless pursuit, the boys finally cornered the silhouetted figure at a dead-end, amidst the stacks of boxes and rows and rows of trash and treasures, back turned to them.

"Chuck, what are you doing, we thought we'd never catch yo-" Billy approached and reached out a hand, touching his friend's shoulder. Almost immediately he let out a yelp, and leapt back as if hit by a lightning bolt.

It was *not* Chuck in his homemade chipmunk costume.

Instead it was, by all accounts, some kind of snarling, odious, oversized chipmunk, unlike anything Billy had ever seen. Anthropomorphic, almost teddy bear-like in appearance, but absent of any cuteness or cuddliness. About four feet in stature, covered in a mangy, dirty, brown pelt. A ravenous countenance, with beady yellow eyes.

The thing smiled at the boys, bearing a full set of very big, very sharp teeth.

CHAPTER 31

A New Terror

T he kids screamed at the sight of the hair-raising crit-
ter before them. Rearing up, the furry menace brandished two clawed-paws, poised to attack, when-

GROWL. A low yet booming rumble echoed again throughout
the basement.

Once ready to pounce, the creature now froze in place, wild-
eyed. An abrupt role reversal, from scary to scared. Letting loose
a timid *squeak*, the thing bolted, scuttling away into the darkness.
Wherever that growl had come from, it wanted no part.

Alarmed yet relieved that they weren't going to be devoured
then and there, the boys took a moment to regain their compos-
ure. It was Germ who broke the silence.

"Can anyone - ANYONE - explain to me what just happened?"
he asked.

"It would appear," offered Phil, "that the small terrifying
thing was scared off by the even bigger, even more frightening
thing."

"Well I can't wait to meet it," snorted Germ.

"I think we might if we don't get out of here," Billy interjected. "Like now."

Their hushed whispers were broken by the faint sound in the distance, of a familiar and gentle voice. A voice that sounded an awful lot like-

"-Chuck?" Billy wondered aloud.

Listening intently, the boys held their breath until they heard the voice again. It was muffled, but there was no mistake.

"It's him!" Phil exclaimed. He scanned the dark basement. "Chuck's down here! The real Chuck."

As fast as they could, the boys took off, running half-crouched so as not to expose themselves. Navigating the twist and turns, overstepping gardening tools and rogue tricycles, they followed the sound of Chuck's voice until Phil had eyes on him.

"Over there!" The boys broke into a run.

Sure enough, in a rusty old cage, glasses askew and faux fur matted, was their dear friend.

Chuck, who had been curled in a ball hugging his knees, was alarmed by the commotion until he saw that the three charging figures were his best friends. Throwing caution aside, he ran to the bars and reached out.

"Guys, it's really you!" Chuck exclaimed.

"Chuck! We need to get you out of there!" Billy whispered.

Chuck shook his head fervently. "No, no, no... *you* need to get in here. Fast."

"Are you nutso?" Germ snapped. "We gotta move. Scram. *Vamanos*. There's some kind of monster out here, Chuckers. And don't even get me started on the chipmunks." Billy gave Germ a stern look which prompted Germ to follow-up. "Uh, and I'm glad you're okay," he added. Chuck smiled.

Almost on cue, the happy reunion was interrupted by a snarling sound.

Chuck froze up, and a look of pure dread spread across his face. Billy turned to see what his friend saw.

Emerging from the shadows was the stuff of childhood nightmares. The thing in the closet watching your every move. The terror under the stairs, personified. A truly gruesome, spine-chilling sight.

It was a monster. Hulking. Scaled and covered in spiky flesh, with giant horns and a skeletal face. It smiled a menacing grin at Billy and the boys, revealing bloodied fangs; teeth that could tear their bodies to pieces with one unceremonious bite.

Casually, the monster tossed what looked to be a carcass over its shoulder. Billy squinted to make out the freshly skinned pelt of an oversized chipmunk. Very similar looking to the mutant chipmunk only recently mistaken for Chuck.

The boys watched on in shocked horror. Salivating, the monster's eyes shone as it surveyed the kids, a potential second course.

"It brings friends, it does. Tasty, tasty friends."

CHAPTER 32

Fluffy

Appetite primed, the monster rounded on the boys, blocking them against the cage.

"I-I tried to tell you," Chuck said, looking utterly helpless. "It's safer in here than out there."

Chuck was most certainly right but, having faced his share of murderous maniacs tonight, Billy swallowed his fear and decided to go with a different, more diplomatic approach.

"Hello, Mister... missus? Er- Your Honorable Monster." Unsure of the right way to address the creature, he figured flattery could be an option.

"You're right; Chuck did bring us here. Little guy went and got himself lost. But now he's found! So we'll get right out of your...er... hair." The other boys nodded emphatically.

"*Stay for dinner... friends,*" the monster extended a massive, spiky limb, blocking Billy's path. "*In fact, multiple may you make dinners for me.*" Steam rushed from its massive nostrils as it spoke.

"Dinner? N-no thank you, we're not hungry..."

"*To start with the fingies, I like...*" Billy abandoned all attempts to reason with the monster, and he cowered alongside his friends as the monster reached out, taking one of Germ's hands in its claws. His hand looked miniscule by comparison, like a doll's. Germ shrieked, and Billy and Phil grabbed his other arm, pulling him back from the beast, however their strength was no match; the monster pulled Germ into its clutches.

Jaw wide, the monster relished the moment, savoring the anticipation between now and the first nibble of fingie. But snacktime was interrupted by a small, trembling voice.

"Hey! Scale-face! Leave him alone. It's m-me you want, so dig in!"

Chuck had stepped out from behind the safety of the cage bars and stood, arms wide, offering himself as human bait. The monster dropped Germ like a sack of bad potatoes.

"No Chuckers!" Germ protested. "Get back in the cage!"

But it was too late -- the monster only had eyes for Chuck.

"*Munk meat!*" It barked.

Chuck moved in front of his friends, creating a shield between them and the monster. The creature, honing in on its prey, charged, grabbing Chuck by the arm, pulling him close. Chuck gave a yelp as its claws grazed his flesh. Still, he put on a brave face and turned to his friends, flashing a pained yet warm smile as the beast sniffed at him.

"Tell Gram that I'll miss her," Chuck said, choking back tears. "And that I only pretended to like liver and onions so she wouldn't feel bad." Wincing, he closed his eyes and braced for impact as the monster bared its fangs, salivating like a dog over a fresh pile of bones.

Helpless, Billy and the other boys watched on in horror, unable to wake from the real life nightmare that was happening before them; their friend about to be eaten alive. When suddenly-

Bop!

In one swift motion, a small and delicate hand reached out from the shadows and struck the monster on its boney snout.

"Bad. Bad!" a familiar voice scolded.

The monster recoiled back in surprise, dropping a dazed Chuck from its clutches. Just as shocked were the other boys when they saw who had so brazenly reprimanded the creature.

It was Vanessa.

"Vanessa… You're alive!" Billy cried out.

"Surprisingly, so are you," she retorted. No longer in her witch costume, she donned the usual shabby, black attire she wore to school.

Germ ran to Chuck's side. "Chuck, are you okay? You risked your life to save us!" he exclaimed, propping up his friend in his arms. Woozy, Chuck pulled back his fur sleeve to reveal a slight scratch on his arm.

"Wounded. But I'll live," he replied, a hint of drama in his voice. Regaining his bearings, Chuck looked up to see Vanessa standing before the creature. "Look out Vanessa, there's a monster-"

"Fluffy, sit," said Vanessa, sternly.

Without hesitation, the monster rolled back on its hind legs, diligently sitting. Within an instant the creature transformed into an obedient puppy dog.

"What did I say about eating the neighbors, Fluffy?"

Fluffy, as it were, cowered in shame. Its scaled tail hung between its legs. The monster replied as if reciting. "*'Human makes not for cuisine too good. Scrawmunk only to eat.'*"

The boys looked on aghast as Vanessa reached into her pocket and pulled out a bloody chunk of meat. She gave it a toss and the monster grabbed it mid-air, swallowing the meat whole.

"Good boy, Fluffy."

"Fluffy?" Billy looked from the monster to Vanessa. "Is this thing a *pet* of yours?"

Vanessa gave the monster a couple affectionate pats on its scaly back. It made a purring sound in return. "It gets lonely living in a big house like this."

The boys gasped.

"Did you just say you live here? In Bryerwood House?" asked Germ.

"Are we hearing you correctly?" pressed Phil.

"... B-but you said you disappeared too! You led us to the basement to search for Chuck!" Billy exclaimed, flabbergasted.

Ignoring the boys and their frantic questions, Vanessa turned to address Fluffy. "Poor baby, you must be hungry. There's a bucket of scrawmunk meat waiting in your den." To that, Fluffy let out a pleased growl.

"Munk meat! Munk meat!" The monster gave Vanessa a slobbery lick on the face, and ran off in search of its meal.

"'Scrawmunk?' Is that what the rabid little furry thing was?" Phil asked.

Vanessa nodded. "Yes. And given his costume," she pointed at Chuck, "you're pretty lucky. The chipmunk and scrawmunk may be distant cousins but to Fluffy they might as well be two courses in the same meal."

Billy shook his head. "Forget the strawmunk - or scrawmunk - whatever it is... You *live* here?" He was absolutely flabbergasted. "So that was all an act?

Vanessa paused. "Yes. Yes it was."

"But you go to our school! And... and you're friends with Sarah!" Billy searched for the words. "You seemed... normal."

Vanessa stared at the ground, silent for a moment.

"You mean I seemed like *your* version of normal," she replied, icily. "Living in your perfect house, on just the right street. Affable parents. Take the family on a vacation once a year, dinner on the table every night. Not a care in the world, except whether or not you can replace the baseball you lost, playing and trespassing on someone else's property."

Billy felt hot in the face and could tell he was flushing bright red. He looked to his friends for their reaction, but saw that Phil and Chuck were both staring at the ground, and Germ was oddly fascinated with his fingernails.

Vanessa went on. "Bryerwood House is all I've ever known. Albeit not perfect, but it's what we have, and it's our home."

"But you're the new kid."

"At school, yes," Vanessa replied. "I begged my dad to let me go to school this year instead of teaching me at home, as he's always done. He warned me that the other kids would view me as strange. My interests, my... *peculiarities*. We're different, but who isn't? And of course, this house. It's a horror to you, because that's what you want it to be. Your stories, your theories. It all came true because it's what you wanted to be true. What you assumed. But it's home to me. And my dad..."

She paused and bit her lip. Typically she excluded an aloof confidence, but this was the first time Billy had seen Vanessa show any sort of crack in her veneer.

"Speaking of my dad, you wouldn't happen to know anything about his serum vial, would you Billy?" Vanessa asked.

Billy thought back to the vial he had knocked over in the

drawing room, spilling its contents on the floor and hastily replacing it with a different liquid. His embarrassment soared. Now, connecting the dots, he realized that the liquid in that vial wasn't just any liquid, but a potion, and a vital one at that.

"He was a scientist once, you know," Vanessa continued, her eyes glazing over as if lost in another train of thought. "Well, technically he still is. A great one, in fact."

There was a long, heavy silence, until Chuck spoke up. "I live with my grandma."

Vanessa's somber expression was replaced with one of piqued interest. "You do?"

"Yeah. Not many kids live with their grandmas, but mine's great. We play lots of card games together, and she lets me steer the car in the cemetery parking lot."

Vanessa raised an eyebrow. "You go to the cemetery with her?"

"Every weekend, to see her friends. Well, except Sally Mesner, Grandma says that's a 'spite visit.'"
Chuck paused, thought to himself a moment, then continued. "You could come with us sometime!"

Brightening, Vanessa gave a small smile. "I would like that."

Chuck returned a sheepish grin, and pushed up his smudged glasses with one hand, the other cradling his scratched arm.

Next Germ stepped forward. "My dad travels. A lot." As he spoke he nervously twisted his fedora in his hands. "Most of the time it's just my mom, Becca and me. He tries to be there for the important stuff, but doesn't always make it. It's cool that your dad is close to you."

Nodding, Vanessa seemed to soften more. "He's a good man." She looked sideways at Billy. "You just caught him at a bad time."

Billy was in the wrong and knew it. He felt ashamed now, thinking back to all the comments he'd made about Bryerwood in front of Vanessa. And those she hadn't heard. He considered how he would feel if someone was mocking or telling rumors about his home and family.

"I'm sorry, Vanessa," he said. "I hope we can be friends."

Vanessa gave a tiny shrug. "Friends are a newer concept for me, but I'm down to give it a shot."

"You said your dad's a scientist?" interjected Phil. "I'm the chair of the junior science club. If he's willing, I could use a mentor. Sometimes it feels like *I'm* the one who's teaching Mr. Pulatzky's in third period Bio."

Vanessa laughed aloud at this. "That's not just you. Mr. Pulatzky's the worst."

This sparked laughter from all. Mr. Pulatzky *was* the worst.

Vanessa clapped her hands twice, and the basement lit up. "I suppose we can't just hang here all night," she said. The boys look around, astonished. Not only did the space seem much less scary, but seeing it now in the light revealed that it was ten times smaller than the shadows and labyrinth of clutter had led them to believe. Sure it was filled with a bunch of strange old stuff, nevertheless it felt kind of like your average basement. Well, aside from the scrawmunk blood splattered on the floor.

"So what now?" Billy asked.

"Now?" Vanessa replied, with a coy smile. "It's time to party."

The boys exchanged confused looks. "... Party?"

"Yes, party." Vanessa winked. "It's Halloween, after all."

CHAPTER 33

It Was the Monster Mash

Following Vanessa closely, the five wove their way out of the basement, Chuck of course keeping a keen eye open for Fluffy on the way. When they got to the main floor, the boys were shocked to see that the party Vanessa alluded to was already underway and Bryerwood House felt like a very different place; a lot had changed, to say the least. Flummoxed, the boys took it all in as they followed Vanessa through the halls.

While still somewhat dark and ramshackle, the house now had a strange sense of "life" to it. The foyer was lit and the many doors once locked were now propped open, and inviting. Magically repaired, the winding staircase was decorated with a garland of dried flowers and leaves wrapping the banister. Soft light illuminated from room-to-room and down every twisting corridor. Flickering candles, pumpkins, and fall foliage adorned tabletops and nooks, bringing a shabby festivity to the place. Strung among the cobwebs were black cloth streamers - fancy ones - not just the crepe kind from the party store. Eerie yet up-tempo music echoed throughout. Indeed, a party was in full-swing. As if the night wasn't unbelieve enough, Bryerwood House was now bustling with the presence of *party goers*.

The bulk of the guests were what Billy could only assume to be ghosts; spectral and lit by an otherworldly blue hue. The kids stopped and peeked in the drawing room. Some of the ghosts were dancing to piano music being played by a pair of floating hands. Alongside them danced some small furry creatures, much more cheerful and pleasant looking than the scrawmunk from earlier. Chuck still tensed up at the sight.

Passing the game room, the boys caught a glimpse of none other than the violent ventriloquist dummy who had terrorized Germ. Now engaged in a poker game with a Wolfman, a giant spider, and a mysterious looking woman cloaked head-to-toe in crimson, the puppet cackled as he raked in a large stack of chips much to the dismay of his companions. Germ gulped when he saw and locked eyes with the doll, however the dummy merely smirked at him and raised his hand, making a playful finger gun gesture. Bewildered, Germ returned it.

The dining room was also full of interesting characters. A tall pale man with gaunt features and black wells for eyes sat at the head of the table, on which a sprawling harvest feast was layed; cheeses and meats, roasted butternut squash, carrots and potato gratin, mushroom soup, seasoned roots, cinnamon rolls and pumpkin pie. Seated to the pale man's left was a stylish gentleman with lush black hair and a widow's peak. When the gentleman smiled you could see his sharp incisors, almost like fangs. As the pale man partook in the feast, gobbling down fistfuls of food at a time, the other man drank from a goblet full of dark red liquid. Also in their company was a two-headed green creature (a woman, if the pigtails were any indication). The identical heads were debating over who would eat the last traces of yorkshire pudding. Billy wondered if they realized that it would eventually end up in the same stomach, but didn't think it was his place to say.

Next to the dining room was a warm, stone laden kitchen, the centerpiece of which was a large iron cauldron hanging above a roaring hearth. A cluster of older women, close to Chuck's grandmother's age, buzzed about the room opening random jars and powders and dropping their contents into the vessel, singing a soothing chant as they did so.

Every room was filled with ghouls, monsters and otherworldly beings, dancing, laughing, and making merry. It occurred to Billy that he should probably feel scared, except the mood was... fun. Everyone was having a good time, and, aside from the odd glance, the boys were met with smiles and nods. Nothing felt threatening about it.

That is until...

Vanessa and the boys arrived at the sitting room where Billy had encountered the strange man earlier in the evening. Sure enough, he was there. Billy was startled at the sight, then quickly he reminded himself that this was Vanessa's father. Spotting his daughter, the man made his way over.

Clearing his throat, he addressed the kids. "Hello everyone. I'm Dr. Delile." He extended a bruised hand which the boys shook one-by-one. Although still slightly disheveled and beat-up from the events of before, he now looked about as harmless as a church mouse.

"And good to see you again, Billy," Dr. Delile added. "We had an... unfortunate introduction before. Allow me to apologize. Usually I take my serum and retreat to my quarters when I feel a 'change' coming on, but what with the party I lost track of time, and-" Dr. Delile put an arm around Vanessa who smiled brightly. "Well, it seems there was an accidental mix-up with my vials."

"Er... I'm sorry, sir," Billy replied.

"Think nothing of it." The doctor waved a hand, as if this was par for the course.

"Your house is very... do you... um... uh... do you..."

"... Have many parties with ghosts, goblins, vampires and monsters?" the doctor laughed. "Not often. In fact, only once a year. On Halloween, Bryerwood House is a crossing point for all sorts of unusual souls."

"You don't say," Germ quipped, half distracted by a gaggle of gremlins tearing at a basket of sour candy.

Vanessa held her arms out, emphatically. "This is my favorite night of the year! And I never get to share it with any friends."

"You do now!" Chuck puffed his chest out and Vanessa looked pleased. Almost as pleased as the punch that the gremlins were now downing, directly from the bowl.

"Splendid!" Dr. Delile clapped his hands together. "Given the... *nature* of our house, Vanessa and I don't have many visitors from the neighborhood. But you boys are always welcome here. And next time you hit a baseball into the yard, give me a call. I've got a helluva curve."

This night couldn't get any stranger, Billy thought. Nevertheless, he... liked it.

"We will!" he replied.

"Come on!" Vanessa beckoned to the boys. "There's a good party going to waste."

And so, Vanessa, Germ, Billy and Chuck made their way to the drawing room to dance. Meanwhile, Phil hung back alongside Dr.

Delile for a moment.

"Dr Delile, may I ask you a question?"

"Of course, what is it? My daughter tells me you're one of the most scientifically gifted students in her class! I'd love to answer any questions you might have."

Phil beamed. "No, it's nothing to do with science. It's-" His gaze drifted to a portrait that hung over the fireplace.

Preserved forever in a gilded bronze frame, was the likeness of a beautiful young woman, with raven hair, wearing a white, lace dress. Around her neck she wore a heart-shaped locket.

"Who," Phil asked, "is that? In the portrait?"

"That," Dr. Delile responded, "is Vanessa's french tutor. Madame Dubois. Our current attic resident."

Phil gulped. "And... how's Vanessa doing with her french?"

"Fantastic now, thanks to Madame. Why do you ask?"

CHAPTER 34

A Happy Halloween

After Phil broke the news about Madame Dubois's untimely end to a very understanding Dr. Delile, he caught up with his friends. Vanessa confessed that she didn't much like french anyway and besides, Madame Dubois could be a bit pushy. Phil was relieved.

From there on, the night was a blur. The kids danced and ate pumpkin delicacies. Drank cider punch. Met all kinds of unusual creatures and characters. Told jokes and stories and laughed until their sides hurt.

It was the most magical Halloween any of them had ever had.

Eventually the party began to dwindle, and the friends found themselves saying their goodbyes at the front door. Before they departed, Vanessa pulled out a large black cauldron. From it, she presented each of the boys with a fantastical piece of Halloween candy, the likes of which they had never seen.

"It's not often we get trick-or-treaters," she said happily, as she distributed the treats. "In fact, it's never."

"You don't say," Germ muttered quietly to himself. Speaking

louder to Vanessa, he said; "consider it tradition. Starting next year yours will be the first house we visit. If we're invited back, of course."

"Sounds good to me. I'll have to talk it over with the dummy though." Vanessa smirked. Germ grinned, enjoying a taste of his own medicine.

"Thanks Vanessa," Chuck said, gnawing on the elaborate candy. "All-in-all, it was a heck of a party. Give Fluffy a belly rub for me."

Phil chimed in. "Agreed. And, if uh, you need any help with french class... don't hesitate to ask."

Billy shuffled his feet and took a deep breath. "Vanessa, this party was..."

"... Awesome?" she smiled. "I know."

Billy smiled back and gave a tip of his helmet and a flourish of his Danger Kevin cape.

Vanessa laughed. "You guys better hurry if you want to get home before it's light out."

CHAPTER 35

Grounded

I t wasn't more than two blocks from Bryerwood House that the foursome encountered Billy's parents who had organized the neighbors in an all-out search party for the "missing" boys. They'd been worried sick, as were Phil's parents, Germ's mom, and Chuck's grandma.

After the boys failed to meet Becca at the designated meeting place and time, she had no choice but to come clean and tell the adults they'd gotten separated. Germ's mother was furious, grounding Becca an additional three weeks on top of the existing hard time she was already doing for her shoplifting transgression.

Any other night this would be music to Germ's ears. But now, looking at a bleary-eyed Becca and feeling ever-changed by his experience in Bryerwood House, he felt a strange new sense of maturity and compassion. Throwing himself on the proverbial fire, he dramatically insisted to his mother that in reality it was his idea to run away from the protective eye of his *very* responsible sister, for the purposes of - as he put it - "nondescript Halloween mischief." Germ's mother listened to his impassioned plea with one eyebrow raised. Sighing, she resignedly split Becca's grounding between her delinquent daughter and son. Social life saved, Becca was eternally grateful. There was a solid week where the siblings got along like old chums, that is until Germ snooped in her diary, and then the truce was off.

Phil's parents were disappointed with the trouble the boys' desertion had caused, but as usual, chalked it up to a learning experience. When Phil asked if he was grounded, his parents looked at each other, unsure how to respond having never found themselves in this position before. Phil suggested that perhaps docking his TV time would be substantial enough. His parents conceded.

Billy's parents were incredibly disappointed in him. He desperately wanted to tell them the truth about the evening at Bryerwood, but was convinced - as understanding as his parents were - that they'd consider it some kind of tall tale. So he took his lumps and didn't protest when he was grounded and assigned sole raking duty for the foreseeable autumn season. He did however tell his parents about his new friend Vanessa, who was "different, but pretty cool." As he described her, Billy couldn't help but notice his mother and father exchanging sly smiles.

Chuck's grandmother showered him in an embarrassing amount of hugs and kisses, and Chuck felt incredibly guilty for making her worry. The next morning he regaled her with stories of Bryerwood House; of Fluffy and the scrawmunk, and the fantastically ghoulish party. His grandmother nodded and laughed, complimenting Chuck on his vivid imagination. Pretending he wasn't, Noogie Nick listened from the living room doorway.

When Chuck made his way to his bedroom that night, he passed an unusually subdued Nick in the hall. Extending an arm,

Nick blocked his path.

"What really happened there?" he grunted, cracking his dirty knuckles.

Every muscle in Chuck's body stiffened. "You heard me," he replied, trying to keep his voice steady.

"Prove it." Nick took another intimidating step forward and glowered down at his brother. Rising to his full height, Chuck wordlessly lifted his sleeve to reveal a souvenir from his altercation with Fluffy.

"Ha! A puny scrape?" Nick spit. "I can give you another one just like it right now, snotface." He advanced on Chuck, but unlike any confrontation that had occurred in the prior thirteen years of Chuck's life, this time the young boy stood his ground.

"You can," Chuck said, his voice void of emotion. "You can hurt me. Bully me. Call me names. Abuse me. Do your worst, Nicholas."

Irate by Chuck's newfound impertinence, Nick raised his hand in a fist, about to strike, but was caught off-guard as Chuck too raised his hand, pointing at something behind his brother.

"I warn you," Chuck continued. "*He'll* do worse to you."

Nick turned to see what Chuck was pointing at.

Hunched outside Nick's bedroom window was a horrible, scaled monster, gleaming in the moonlight. It raised one powerful, long limb and gave Chuck a clawed wave, which the boy gleefully returned. Then, honing in on Nick, the creature bared its teeth in a menacing smile.

Nick's eyes grew wide and he fell back against the hallway wall, shaking in tremendous fear.

"That's Fluffy," Chuck said, cold as ice, stepping over his downed and trembling brother. "And he's with me."

Confident as ever, Chuck strode to his room, head held high. Noogie Nick never bullied his brother again.

CHAPTER 36

Baseball

As the boys served their respective sentences at home, they still found time to socialize and have fun during school lunch hours. These now included Vanessa, who fit in so naturally that it was difficult to remember a time when she wasn't one of the gang. She didn't lose her quirk though, and every once in a while she'd make a remark that left the boys scratching their heads (instant classics such as, "bats make great pets," and "shovels are literally a groundbreaking invention."). On top of that, she was an endless well of magpie facts, which Phil found fascinating.

Above all, Billy, Chuck, Germ and Phil admired Vanessa's unique taste and strong sense of self. Being friends with Vanessa was a daily demonstration of how to feel happy in your own skin, and the boys themselves grew because of it.

After some awkward apologizing for her swift departure on Halloween night, Sarah also became a mainstay of the friend group, joining for activities like ice skating, movie nights, and some raucous snowball fights. After some time, Vanessa confided in Sarah and brought her home to Bryerwood House, which eventually evolved into Sarah being a regular at Vanessa's after school. She even offered to adopt one of Fluffy's litter, however Vanessa didn't think Sarah's parents would be as open-minded to a scaled monster as their daughter was, so the offer was politely declined.

The months passed and the events of Halloween became a distant memory, one that gained a fonder spin with each retelling. Fall turned to winter and winter turned to spring. And then, as if it had never left, baseball season was once again in session.

On a clear spring weekend, the gang gathered for their first game. Not at the park, even though Noogie Nick was no longer a threat, but instead returning to the empty lot beside Bryerwood House.

"Get ready for the heat." Billy tipped the brim of his hat and drew his glove up, tightening his pitching stance.

"Do your worst, I'm feeling a bit chilly!" Germ taunted from home plate. He put a hand to the side of his mouth and called out in the direction of third base. "Get ready Chuckers, I'm sending you home, buddy!"

Billy checked the runner on third, Chuck, who was distracted from the game and playing hopscotch with the base. Hearing his name, Chuck looked up and responded with a thumbs-up. "I'm on it!"

"Save some room for me there!" Vanessa called out as she dusted her jeans off from a pretty epic slide into first.

Billy gritted his teeth and kneaded his glove, looking to the catcher, Sarah, for her signal. Three balls up, Germ was at risk of being walked to first. Sarah gave Billy the sign for a fastball. Billy nodded.

He wound up, transferring all the energy and momentum he

had into this single pitch. The ball flew fast, like a torpedo targeted for home plate.

Germ lasered his sights on the ball. Focused, he swung with all his might, and the bat connected, dead-on.

CRACK. The ball burst upward from Germ's swing, like a rocket taking flight above the field. Billy reached up and made an attempt, but it was too high to catch.

Sprinting at full speed, Vanessa was at second base in no time. As she rounded for third she caught the attention of Chuck, who jumped and broke into a run for home. Germ trailed behind in a jog, admiring his swing.

Billy watched as the ball soared higher overhead. Far in the outfield, fighting against a blindingly bright sun, Phil raised a gloved fist and tracked the ball, doing his best to get beneath it.

But it was going... going...

Gone.

The ball cleared the fence, leaving the field, and disappearing behind the brush of trees in the Bryerwood backyard.

The kids stopped in astonishment, gawking at one another. Silence. Until...

"... I'll get it!" Germ exclaimed, breaking into a run toward the house.

"No, I'll get it!" Billy exclaimed, chased after him.

"It's my house!" Vanessa laughed.

"Race you for it!" Chuck called out, breathless already.

Soon all six of the friends were racing to see who could make it to Bryerwood House first. It marked the start of an unforgettable summer, and only two hundred and three days until the next Halloween.

END

ACKNOWLEDGEMENT

Thank you to my husband James who bolsters me when I lack confidence, tolerates my madness, and cheers me on without fail. The story of my life is best written beside you.

Thank you to the friends who have given me support and encouraged me along the way.

Thank you to my parents who in my youth wouldn't buy me video games, but took me to the library any time I asked.

ABOUT THE AUTHOR

Elyse Willems

Elyse Willems is a writer, producer, performer, and creative based in Los Angeles, California. She was born and raised in exotic Toronto, Canada, a snowy wonderland known for molding and churning out funny weirdos. Spending time with her husband James and dog Benson brings Elyse endless joy.

Her favorite childhood book is "The Westing Game."

photo by: J Finger

Printed in Great Britain
by Amazon